Mask
–of the–
Wolf Boy

Trailblazer Books

Gladys Aylward • *Flight of the Fugitives*
Mary McLeod Bethune • *Defeat of the Ghost Riders*
William & Catherine Booth • *Kidnapped by River Rats*
Governor William Bradford • *The Mayflower Secret*
John Bunyan • *Traitor in the Tower*
Amy Carmichael • *The Hidden Jewel*
Peter Cartwright • *Abandoned on the Wild Frontier*
Elizabeth Fry • *The Thieves of Tyburn Square*
Jonathan & Rosalind Goforth • *Mask of the Wolf Boy*
Sheldon Jackson • *The Gold Miners' Rescue*
Adoniram & Ann Judson • *Imprisoned in the Golden City*
Festo Kivengere • *Assassins in the Cathedral*
David Livingstone • *Escape from the Slave Traders*
Martin Luther • *Spy for the Night Riders*
Dwight L. Moody • *Danger on the Flying Trapeze*
Samuel Morris • *Quest for the Lost Prince*
George Müller • *The Bandit of Ashley Downs*
John Newton • *The Runaway's Revenge*
Florence Nightingale • *The Drummer Boy's Battle*
Nate Saint • *The Fate of the Yellow Woodbee*
Menno Simons • *The Betrayer's Fortune*
Mary Slessor • *Trial by Poison*
Hudson Taylor • *Shanghaied to China*
Harriet Tubman • *Listen for the Whippoorwill*
William Tyndale • *The Queen's Smuggler*
John Wesley • *The Chimney Sweep's Ransom*
Marcus & Narcissa Whitman • *Attack in the Rye Grass*
David Zeisberger • *The Warrior's Challenge*

Also by Dave and Neta Jackson

Hero Tales: A Family Treasury of True Stories
From the Lives of Christian Heroes (Volumes I, II, & III)

Mask –of the– Wolf Boy

Dave & Neta Jackson

Story illustrations by
Julian Jackson

BETHANY HOUSE PUBLISHERS
MINNEAPOLIS, MINNESOTA 55438

Published by Bethany House Publishers
A Ministry of Bethany Fellowship International
11400 Hampshire Avenue South
Minneapolis, Minnesota 55438
www.bethanyhouse.com

Printed in the United States of America by
Bethany Press International, Minneapolis, Minnesota 55438

ISBN 0–7642–2011–X

Chou Fu-lin is a fictional character. However, he coincides with three historical persons. The Goforths did have a servant who fled their caravan at Fancheng when he heard of the plot against the missionaries. He returned to Changte to report that everyone had been killed. Years later, a "Wolf Boy" (given that name for the same reasons we gave it to Fu-lin) was a childhood playmate of Mary Goforth. Mary remembers that he was the son of one of Mrs. Goforth's "Bible women." (A Bible woman was a trusted personal assistant to women missionaries, skilled enough in the Scriptures to be able to teach.) Finally, there was a young Christian (no other identification mentioned) who at first couldn't find the Goforths a place to rent in the town of Hotsun, but at the last minute when the crowd was pressing in, he went out a second time and succeeded.

Though the real Wolf Boy was probably younger than we have made Fu-lin, he never complained about the event that led to his nickname because, as he said, "Without it, I never would have heard about Jesus."

Except for the direct interactions with Fu-lin, all other events involving the Goforths actually happened. One thing is out of sequence: Ruth's escape from contracting smallpox after playing all day with an infected child actually happened a few years later to Mary, who was not yet born at this time.

DAVE AND NETA JACKSON are a husband/wife writing team who have authored and coauthored many books on marriage and family, the church, and relationships, including the books accompanying the Secret Adventures video series, the Pet Parables series, the Caring Parent series, and the newly released *Hero Tales,* Volumes I, II, and III.

The Jacksons have two married children: Julian, the illustrator for TRAILBLAZER BOOKS, and Rachel, who has recently blessed them with a granddaughter, Havah Noelle. Dave and Neta make their home in Evanston, Illinois.

CONTENTS

Chapter 1

A Bad Way to End a Funeral

H E WAS FALLING, FALLING, FALLING amid dirt and sticks and dried leaves. Down, down, his arms flailing, like swimming down into the dark. Then— *whap!* His shoulder hit a stone sticking out from the wall. He tumbled forward to crash headlong into the dust of the cave's floor—

Chou Fu-lin awoke from his dream, panting heavily. The smell was still there, like something rotten and soaked in urine. Fear gripped him. It was not just falling down into the cave; something much worse was about to happen. He could sense it. He choked back a cry for help. He knew it would do no good. Besides, if he woke the

9

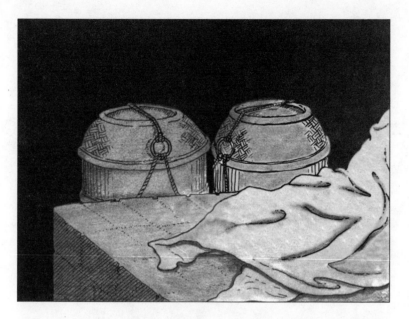

others, they might see him without his mask. It seemed he always had these dreams when something awful was happening. What would it be this time?

And then he remembered. He already knew. Today was the day they were going to bury the body of seven-year-old Florence Goforth, so small, so innocent with her golden curly hair. What could be worse than a funeral for a child? And yet Fu-lin could not escape the sense of dread that something even worse *would* happen, and soon. His fear was as strong as the smell that hung around him like an unseen cloud. When he'd had these dreams at home, he had asked his mother about the smell, but she could never smell it. "It is just the wolf," she'd say. "Now go back to sleep."

This time the smell was so strong that Fu-lin checked to see that he had not wet himself. But he was dry. Maybe a slight breeze had blown into the house from the open sewer that ran down the middle of the street.

Fu-lin lay in the hot room on the hard *kang*, the large brick platform that served as a bed, and waited for morning. Its faint light streamed through the window as his thoughts drifted back over the past two years, when he had come to these strange foreigners at the age of twelve. Since then he had served in their home in exchange for a place to live and free schooling at the missionary school. Ever since his father died, Fu-lin's family had been too poor to pay the tuition to keep him in school. So he had worked. It was a good arrangement, the only way he could continue getting an education. But he often got lonely for his younger sister, little twin brothers, and especially his mother.

After waiting a long while, Fu-lin heard quiet noises from the adjoining room. Then, around the edge of the tattered blanket that served as the door between the two sleeping rooms, he saw a faint glow. Fu-lin knew what was happening: Mr. Goforth had lit his lamp. First he would do his "daily dozen" exercise routine, and then he would take the lamp into the sitting room to begin his morning prayers and Bible reading. Even on the day of his daughter's funeral, he had not changed his routine.

This was not the first funeral the missionary from Canada had performed for one of his own children. Fu-lin had heard more than once how the Goforths had lost baby Gertrude before she was a year old. And then wee Donald—nothing but a toddler—had fallen off the porch and hit his head on a flowerpot. At first there was only a big lump on his head, but then he became unable to use his arms and legs and, in a few days, died. And finally, three-year-old Grace had died of malaria.

But Florence was no infant. At seven years old, she had seemed strong and full of energy until she came down with that awful fever. Now four children were dead, four still living. It was not an uncommon experience in China, but that didn't make it any easier.

With Jonathan Goforth getting up, Fu-lin got up, as well, even though the sun had not yet risen. He put on his thin shirt, wrapped his bandana-like mask around his face and tied it, and went out the back door. The early morning air was only slightly cooler than midday. He looked up at the pale, clear sky. Would it ever rain again? This was a very hot summer and a very long drought. He made his way across the yard to the charcoal bin under the shelter of a small thatched roof. Beside it was the bucket—just as he had left it the evening before—and Fu-lin filled it mechanically with the pressed bricks of charcoal and trudged back to the house. Hauling water from the town fountain and charcoal from the bin and building the cooking fires were some of Fu-lin's jobs, and just now he was glad to be doing anything to get his mind off the haunting dream that had awakened him.

However, even though the "smell" was finally gone, he couldn't get his mind off the dreadful fear that something terrible was going to happen. As much as he told himself that it was just the dread of little Florence's funeral, he felt as if something else was going to happen. Something far worse—if that was possible!

Jonathan Goforth may not have altered his morning routine just because this was a funeral day, but when Fu-lin returned to the house and entered the kitchen, he soon noticed that everyone else seemed different. When Mrs. Goforth came shuffling into the kitchen, she looked like she hadn't slept at all. Her eyes were red, and the smile was missing from her face. She carried baby Wallace on her hip, but he would not be comforted by her jostling and whimpered with a frown bigger than life. Two-and-a-half-year-old Ruth clung to Mrs. Goforth's skirts, almost tripping Mrs. Goforth as she walked.

"Paul, would you come in here and hold Wallace so I can get some breakfast started?" asked Mrs. Goforth in English.

Around the mission station, the Goforths usually spoke Chinese, but occasionally they used English for personal comments to one another or when they were having a private conversation. Fu-lin actually understood English quite well, having studied it in school and practiced it with nine-year-old Paul, but he did not remind the Goforths that their comments weren't so private. This time he ducked his head and busied himself with starting the fire. He did not want to get drafted into baby-sitting duty. He had his jobs, and they didn't include comforting a fussy baby.

"Paul," Rosalind Goforth's voice gained a bite even if it was no louder, "come take the baby!"

Paul slid off the stool by the lamp and came walking across the room, holding the illustrated adventure book ever closer to his eyes the farther he got from the light. "Why can't Helen take William?" he asked absently as he tried to continue reading.

"Because she felt sick in the night, and I don't want another child to . . ." Her voice trailed off at the reference to Florence, whose small body lay in a crude box in the sitting room waiting for burial. "Put that book down and help with your brother," she ordered.

"Paul." The single word came from the sitting

room, where Mr. Goforth was preparing for the funeral. Paul tossed the book back on his stool without even trying to finish his sentence.

As he reached for his baby brother, Mrs. Goforth said, "Thank you!" and then added more kindly, "Nurse Chang will be here soon to help."

Fu-lin finished starting the fire and left to fetch water. The Goforth house was not a place he wanted to spend any more time than necessary, at least not this morning. He put the yoke across his shoulders with a wooden bucket hanging from each end, then hurried off down the street.

The city of Changte was waking up, and in this time of drought, one had to get to the fountain early or the stream would slow to a trickle. But apparently others had the same idea, and Fu-lin had to wait in line for his turn.

"Wolf Boy," said a scratchy voice behind him, "do you still work for those white devils?"

He turned around and recognized Mrs. Feng, an old friend of his mother's. "Yes, honorable Grandmother. I am still going to the mission school," he answered. The old woman was not his real grandmother, but he used the term of respect so the feisty old woman would not become angry.

"I'm sure it makes your poor mother very sad. You'd better leave while you have a chance . . . if you know what's good for you."

"Why is that, Grandmother?"

Her eyes got very large, and she tipped back her head to look down her nose at Fu-lin, even though she was shorter than he was. "The Boxers are coming!" She nearly spat the words at him. "They will drive the white devils out of our land and kill all their supporters! And YOU are one of them!" Then she spun around and shuffled off down the street. "I will take no pleasure in telling your poor mother of your fate," she called back.

After the dream he'd had the night before, this strange warning left Fu-lin shaken. His legs felt so weak that he put down his buckets. He had heard about the Boxers.

Over the years many European nations and Russia and Japan had tried to gain control over various parts of China, grabbing property and privileges and taking unfair advantage of the Chinese people. Naturally, many Chinese were very angry at this bullying. Some believed that Christian missionaries encouraged and supported these activities or at least caused the people to accept foreigners more easily. Their solution was to get rid of *all* foreigners, beginning with the defenseless missionaries. The Chinese Dowager (or widowed) Empress favored this plan and encouraged a secret society of men who called themselves the "righteous, harmonious fists," or Boxers, to kill or throw out all foreigners.

Throughout the spring of 1900, the Boxers had stirred up riots against missionaries and even the Chinese Christians in some cities to the northeast. Even though those problems were miles away, Fu-lin had seen some posters in Changte urging people to kill foreigners and destroy their homes and businesses. But he had not taken the threats seriously. The Boxers did not concern him. Or did they?

He stared after old Mrs. Feng as she wove her way through the growing number of people on the street. Not until she was out of sight did he realize that it was his turn at the fountain.

He picked up his buckets, filled them, and hurried back to the mission station.

That afternoon Fu-lin gathered with the Goforths, Nurse Chang and her mother—old Mrs. Chang, the Bible woman—and Elder Ho from the local Chinese church as they stood by the new grave in the red dirt of the Goforths' backyard. Beside the new grave were the little graves of the other Goforth children.

With a bowed head and a quiet voice, Jonathan Goforth said in Chinese, "It was the apostle Paul himself who said that while 'we are at home in the body, we are absent from the Lord. . . . We are confident . . . and willing rather to be absent from the body, and to be present with the Lord.' He even said that he himself had 'a desire to depart, and to be with Christ; which is far better.' Therefore, as much as we loved our dear Florence, we can take comfort in believing God's Word that on this day, June 20, 1900, she is in a far better place than she was yesterday before she died."

He stopped and swallowed hard, having difficulty speaking.

Other family members made a few remarks, but Fu-lin couldn't speak. He was still gripped with the sense that bad things were just beginning. Finally Elder Ho prayed, and everyone went inside the house to visit quietly with one another until the evening meal was ready.

Fu-lin always ate alone because of his mask. It was awkward to pull it away from his face whenever he took a bite, but at least no one stared at him. When everyone else was in the other room, he heard a rustling at the door. He hurried to see who was there before the person knocked so the family would not be disturbed. It was a messenger with a packet of letters. Fu-lin took them and was just closing the heavy black door when he called out to the messenger, "Wait a minute. These letters are the ones Mr. Goforth sent out a week ago. They are not *for* him. They were *from* him."

The messenger bowed slightly. "If he doesn't want them, he can burn them."

"No, you don't understand," said Fu-lin. "He wrote these letters. See, there are English words on them because some are to go outside China."

The messenger sighed deeply as he glanced cautiously up and down the street. "Mr. Goforth is very fortunate to have his letters returned," he said in a hushed voice. "The Boxers have stopped all mail from foreigners at the city of Tientsin. There's nothing I can do." He shrugged and walked away.

Reluctantly, Fu-lin took the letters to Mr. Goforth and explained why they had been returned. The missionary shuffled through the stack of letters with a frown on his face. "It seems things are getting worse in the North. Here in Changte we have much to be thankful for."

However, his reminder to be thankful did not lift the heaviness of the day's sad event. There was an empty place at the table, and everyone felt it, even Fu-lin, who ate in the other room.

Two days later when the family was again sitting at the table eating their bowls of steaming rice and vegetables, there was a knock at the door. Mr. Goforth called to Fu-lin, "Would you please answer the door, Fu-lin?"

Fu-lin felt it was an honor to be asked to answer the door. It showed that Mr. Goforth no longer considered him just a child.

The same messenger waited at the door, this time with a wide grin on his face. "Ah, Wolf Boy," he said, holding up a long, very official-looking letter sealed with red wax and adorned with several ornate stamps. "Today Mr. Goforth gets mail from someone other than himself. It comes from the American Consul in Chefoo," he added, pointing to the seal. "The road to Chefoo is still open."

It was necessary to be respectful to his elders, but Fu-lin found the messenger hard to honor. The man had no business paying attention to where people's mail came from or where it went. He was just supposed to deliver it. Fu-lin was about to say something when he realized that someone had come up beside him. He looked up to see Mr. Goforth standing there.

"What do you mean, 'The road to Chefoo is *still* open'?" said the missionary. "Why shouldn't it be open? It hasn't rained in weeks. Anyone ought to be able to cross the Yellow River at almost any point."

"Oh, it's not the river, honorable sir," said the messenger. "It's the Boxers. They are sweeping the country to free us from the white devils." Then he quickly bowed with his hands together as though in prayer. "Begging your pardon, most honorable sir, as we all know, you are a *good* white devil."

"Yes, yes," said Mr. Goforth, bowing his head and handing the messenger a small coin. "Good evening," he added as he closed the door.

Back at the table, Mr. Goforth tore open the letter and read it with frown lines growing deeper in his forehead.

"What is it, Jonathan?" asked Mrs. Goforth.

He answered in English: "The American Consul in Chefoo is advising us and all missionaries to flee. It seems the Boxers are truly on the move. Until now there has been only scattered unrest, but now . . ." He shook his head as his voice trailed off.

"When did they send it?" asked Mrs. Goforth, still speaking in English.

Mr. Goforth turned the letter over and found the date. "Several days ago," he said. "Even this letter was delayed."

"Maybe that is good news," said his wife.

"How could it be?" said Jonathan. "It's probably the unrest that caused the delay."

"Yes," said Rosalind, "but if nothing more has happened by now, maybe it isn't as bad as the Americans thought."

"Possibly," said Mr. Goforth, stroking his short white beard. "I appreciate the Americans' suggestions, but fortunately, as Canadians, we do not have to do what they say. I think things are settling down. Besides, we are a lot closer to the people than those officials in Chefoo, and they respect us." Then slipping back into Chinese, he added, "Why, that fellow at the door just informed me that I am 'one of the *good* white devils.' Now, what do you think of that, Rosalind?" A big grin spread across his face. "Would you agree?"

"You might qualify," said Mrs. Goforth. "I'll have to keep a closer account."

Fu-lin was glad to see a little humor returning to the Goforth home after the death of Florence, but he was not so sure that things were settling down. He still had not been able to shake the feeling that something worse was going to happen.

Chapter 2

The Sign of the Burnt Feather

As SOON AS FU-LIN ARRIVED at the storefront for the usual Friday night prayer meeting, he knew something wasn't right. Like all services, the prayer meeting also served as an evangelistic service where newcomers could hear the Gospel and give their lives to Christ. But when Fu-lin and Mrs. Goforth and the children got to the little church building, paper shades were drawn over the tall front windows, and only a dim light shone through.

Inside, Fu-lin did not see any newcomers, and instead of the women sitting on one side and the men on the other, the few faithful members who were present had drawn chairs into a circle near the front. One small lamp provided light.

"We won't need the organ this evening," said Jonathan to his wife. "Come on up and join us."

"What's happening?" she asked in alarm. This was definitely not the usual type of service.

"When Elder Ho and I arrived a while ago, there were several Boxer posters plastered across the front of the building."

Mrs. Goforth clasped her hand to her mouth in alarm.

"I think we ought to talk about the situation," said Jonathan. He then went on to explain how he had received a second message from the American Consul in Chefoo advising all missionaries to leave and go south because of Boxer activity in the North and East.

"Oh yes, we heard about that," muttered two or three of the Chinese Christians as they looked at the floor and shook their heads.

A brief frown passed over Mr. Goforth's face as he glanced at Nurse Chang and Fu-lin. They were the only two Chinese people in the Goforths' house who might have passed on that information, and Fu-lin knew that he had not told anyone. Then Jonathan Goforth shrugged slightly as though he didn't really care if others had heard.

"Well," he continued, "Rosalind and I have discussed it, and we are not in favor of running like scared rabbits. Other than a few posters and an occasional nasty remark, things have remained peaceful here in Changte. There doesn't seem any cause for panic."

"But bad things are happening elsewhere," interrupted a young man who was a recent convert. "They might spread to Changte. I'm even sorry to say that I think my uncle may be a member of this Boxer society. And he has urged my father to disinherit me for becoming a Christian."

"When the Gospel is effective, there will always be opposition, even persecution," countered Mr. Goforth. "That is why God's Word urges us to take up the shield of faith, so we can quench all of Satan's fiery darts. It's when we are welcomed with nothing but open arms that we should worry. Satan doesn't want to give up any territory."

"Begging your pardon, most honorable teacher, but things may be more serious than we realize," offered Elder Ho in a quiet voice. His sad eyes never seemed to blink. "There have been several attacks on Christians in Chuwang. It may be wise for us to become invisible for a while."

"Hmm," said Mr. Goforth doubtfully. "If things were all that bad in Chuwang, I should think Dr. McKenzie would have notified me before this." Dr. McKenzie and his wife were missionaries in a neighboring town.

"But, Jonathan," said Mrs. Goforth, "what if he is unable to get word to us?"

"We must not speculate about things for which we have no evidence," said Mr. Goforth with a wave of his hand. "It will only lead to panic. I intend to

stay right here and face whatever we must suffer for
our Lord right along with the rest of you."

There was silence in the room as the people considered what their missionary had said. Fu-lin looked around to see how people were responding. Most were looking at the floor.

Suddenly Fu-lin's nose began to itch, and he knew he was about to sneeze. Sneezing can be embarrassing for anyone, but for a young person who wore a mask so people wouldn't see his face, it could be a real problem. A big enough sneeze could blow away the mask. Even small ones were hard to manage.

"Ah-ah-ah-choo!" he exploded less than a second after he got his hand up inside his mask to cover his mouth. Everyone turned to look at him. Perhaps they were glad for a break in the meeting's tension. But it was old Mrs. Chang, the Bible woman, who finally spoke up.

"We appreciate your loyalty to us, Brother Goforth," she said, looking him right in the eye, "and we know you would never abandon us no matter how terrible the threat, but if your own people are advising you to flee, that would seem wise to us. We have discussed this matter," she concluded as though the affair was settled.

"We want you alive so you can return to us when the danger has passed," added Elder Ho. "If necessary, we can become invisible to save our lives . . . but not with you around."

Rosalind Goforth's eyes widened. "Are you saying that our presence makes it more dangerous for you?"

"Please forgive me," said Elder Ho, "but that is true. As foreigners, you are recognizable everywhere."

Rosalind looked at her husband, and he slowly nodded his head in understanding. Drawing in a long, deep breath, he said, "Well, then, we will prepare to depart as soon as possible. It . . . will not be an easy task."

In the days that followed, all the believers pitched in to help the Goforths prepare for their trip. On Saturday while packing began at home, Fu-lin went with Mr. Goforth and Elder Ho to find carts and drivers to take them on the long journey south. "We'll need several carts," Jonathan said to Elder Ho. "I intend to take everything we care about because I don't want any of you worrying about protecting our possessions while we're gone."

But carts and drivers were not so easy to find. Some drivers didn't want to carry the missionaries anywhere, possibly out of sympathy to the Boxer cause or maybe out of fear of the Boxers for helping foreigners. It took until the middle of the afternoon to line up seven carts, drivers, and mules.

When the carts arrived at the mission station, Fu-lin's job was to remove the bamboo mats that covered the hoops over the wagons and replace them with several thick quilts. Once the quilts were secure, he put the bamboo mats over the top of them. "No doubt the heat from the sun will cook us if we are not protected," said Mrs. Goforth as she showed Fu-lin what she wanted him to do. "Besides, this may be the best way to carry our bedding."

Sunday was a day of rest and worship, but every other daylight hour was used in preparation. On Monday evening as Fu-lin ate in the kitchen, he overheard the conversation around the table in the next room. Mrs. Goforth said, "We'll need help on our trip. Would you be willing to come with us, Nurse Chang?"

Fu-lin could barely hear her quiet voice as she agreed to make the difficult journey.

"Thank you," said Mrs. Goforth. "And, Jonathan, have you thought of anyone else?"

"Oh, take Fu-lin! Take Fu-lin," urged Paul eagerly. "He can do a lot of things."

"We can't do that," responded Mrs. Goforth gently. Everyone knew that young Paul looked up to the Chinese boy. "Mrs. Chou would never allow it. So, Jonathan, is there someone else?"

Fu-lin could not help himself. He went to the door and said, "Excuse me, honorable sir, but I would be glad to ask my mother. Such a journey would be very important to my education. I have studied geography very hard, but I have never traveled far from Changte."

Mr. Goforth, sitting at the head of the table, shrugged his shoulders. "Why not?" he said. "It never hurts to ask."

But it was not until Tuesday evening that Fu-lin

was able to leave the mission to seek his mother's permission. When he reached her house, he discovered that Mrs. Goforth was right about how his mother would respond. "Such a long trip is out of the question," she said. "I can't allow my oldest son to go so far away in such uncertain times. How would you get back? With whom would you travel?"

"I would come back with the cart drivers and Nurse Chang," Fu-lin said with confidence, having thought of all the answers as he walked across the city to the Chou family home. "It will be very educational. I will see Kaifengfu, the capital, and the Yellow River, and even Shanghai."

"Shanghai?" Mrs. Chou spat the word. "It has become a western city. Why would anyone want to make a long trip in such hot weather to see a dirty city like Shanghai?"

"Have you been there before, Mother?" asked Fu-lin.

"Well, no, but . . ." Her voice trailed off.

Fu-lin had not meant to embarrass her, so he changed the subject. "Just think, Mother, I might even see the ocean. Now *that's* something worth seeing, isn't it?"

"I suppose so," said his mother. "But here in Changte everyone is used to seeing my son the Wolf Boy. But among strangers . . ." Her dark eyes betrayed the worry she carried for her son who wore the mask. "There could be danger on the road from bandits . . . or these Boxers we keep hearing about." She looked at Fu-lin for several long moments; then her voice dropped to a whisper. "You will come back, won't you?"

His mother had given in to his request! "Without question, most honorable Mother," he said with so much glee that he thought he would burst. "Thank you. Thank you!"

Fu-lin stayed overnight to help around the house and to have time to say good-bye to his little sister and younger twin brothers. Late the next morning he headed back to the mission station—just one day before the caravan was to depart.

A joyful bounce in Fu-lin's step sped him through the crowded streets of Changte on his way back to the mission. He, the Wolf Boy of Changte, was going on a trip, a long journey, a dangerous adventure. He would come back more knowledgeable and better traveled than anyone his age—more experienced, in fact, than many adults.

His excitement had just about driven away his fear of "worse things to come" when a thunderous rumble in the street behind him caused him to spin around. Children began screaming as their mothers hurried them to the side. Rickshaw drivers pulled their carriages out of the way, and everyone looked at the huge black horse galloping at full speed down the street. Snorting and blowing lather, it skidded to a stop in a cloud of dust right in front of Changte's finest inn.

Down from the saddle swung what looked like an imperial warrior in full uniform with a long, curved sword at his side. He tossed the reins of his horse to the inn's groom and barked an order: "Give him the best care and have him ready to ride for Kaifengfu within an hour!" And then he strode into the inn. But just before he disappeared out of sight, Fu-lin noticed a long, white goose feather sticking out of the man's cap. The edge of the feather was burned brown.

Fu-lin's sense of approaching doom came rushing back, like water released from a dam. He knew what that meant. Any official with a burnt feather in his hat carried a message of death from the Dowager Empress. The old Chinese proverb rang in Fu-lin's ears: *"Where the burnt feather goes, death awaits!"*

Chapter 3

The Cowardly Defenders

BREATHLESSLY FU-LIN RAN into the mission compound yelling, "Mr. Goforth! Mr. Goforth!" When he finally found the missionary in the courtyard loading boxes into one of the carts, he shouted, "Where death goes, feathers burn!— I mean—" He stopped, trying to get the proverb straight. "Where the burnt feather goes, death awaits!"

"What?" asked the startled missionary, almost dropping the heavy box. "What are you saying, son?"

"We can't go there!" blurted out Fu-lin. "Where the burnt feather goes, death awaits! It's an old proverb, and we can't go that way."

"Calm down, now. Calm down," said Mr. Goforth

as he finally succeeded in pushing the box into the cart and turned to place his hand on the boy's shoulder. "You aren't making any sense. Why don't you start over and tell me what the problem is?"

Fu-lin took a deep breath and began again more slowly. "I was coming through the city when an imperial messenger came riding down the street. I overheard him say he was going to Kaifengfu, and he had a burnt feather in his cap, so we can't go there."

"I still don't understand," said the missionary. "What's a burnt feather have to do with anything?"

"There's an old proverb that says, 'Where the burnt feather goes, death awaits!' " explained Fu-lin. "Whenever an imperial messenger wears a burnt feather in his cap, it means that he carries a death order. If he's going to Kaifengfu, he's probably on his way to see the governor of the whole Province of Honan. It's got to be a death order for all foreigners. The Empress is the one behind the Boxers. Everyone says so."

"I see," said Mr. Goforth, scratching the bald spot on the top of his head as he looked off into the distance.

"That's why we can't go there," said Fu-lin. "It would be certain death to go through the capital."

"Yes, but we can't go north or east. . . ." Jonathan Goforth's voice trailed off.

Glad for the knowledge he'd learned from books about the local geography, Fu-lin had an idea. "Honorable sir, we could go west until we got into the foothills, and then we could go south and cross the

Yellow River near Chengchow. That would keep us many miles away from Kaifengfu."

"Yes, yes," mused Mr. Goforth, continuing to scratch his head. "That might work, but it would add a couple of days to our trip at least."

The new plans were interrupted by the sounds of carts and mules arriving outside the compound. Fulin opened the gates to find Dr. McKenzie and his family from Chuwang with three carts of their belongings. The Goforth children came running out, and soon everyone was greeting each other and expressing thankfulness for God's protection.

But not an hour had gone by when a young man came pounding on the door. He was dirty, his clothes were torn, and he was covered with sweat. A large wound oozed blood from his scalp.

"It's our servant!" gasped Mrs. McKenzie. "Whatever has happened to you?"

The servant was hustled into the house and his wound attended to as he told his story. As soon as the McKenzies had left their home in Chuwang, Boxers had invaded the house and destroyed or looted all their property. "There was nothing I could do," the young man moaned. "I tried to stop them, but they beat me and threw me out into the street."

Dr. McKenzie quickly assured the young man that he had done all he could and said they would be glad to take him with them to Shanghai. "We can use your help on the trip, and you might find work there," the missionary added. "At least you won't have to return to Chuwang until this trouble has passed."

That evening, many of the local believers gathered at the Goforths' house for a farewell meal. There were many tears and reassurances, and the evening ended with prayer for the safety of those traveling and those staying behind.

"One more thing," said Mr. Goforth after the prayer ended and everyone prepared to leave. "If trouble comes, I don't want any of you to try to protect *this* mission compound. You've heard what happened in Chuwang. We're taking with us any material goods we value, so there'll be nothing here to protect. Please, don't endanger yourselves. We value your lives."

As the door closed on the last Chinese believer, everyone had the same question: Was this their final good-bye?

That night, Fu-lin's sleep was once again disturbed by his old dream. He was falling down, down into a cave, dark, dusty, rotten smelling. Death was all around. His shoulder hit the wall with a terrible blow, and he tumbled, in slow motion, until he flopped like a rag doll on the dusty floor, choking and coughing. He heard a snapping and growling, and through the gloom and dust, amber eyes and white fangs snarled at him with an evil hatred. He was the intruder, and he would have to pay. The worst was coming, and it would be terrible—

Fu-lin awoke, panting and crossing his arms over

his face to protect himself. It was dark. The strong smell seemed to linger around him, as sickening as ever. He coughed and thought for a moment that he was going to throw up.

He held himself as still as possible, and slowly, very slowly, his panting diminished, and he realized that he was safe—for the moment, at least—in the Goforths' house. The rest of the children were sleeping not far from him on the hard kang, but soon everyone would have to rise and prepare to depart on their long journey.

The dream seemed to warn him: Something worse will follow! What would it be? Would he survive? He shook with fear as the foul smell seemed to linger in his nostrils. Maybe . . . maybe he shouldn't go on this trip. Maybe he should slip out of the Goforths' house and go back to his mother's house. But he felt paralyzed and couldn't move.

Shortly before daybreak the next morning, a caravan of ten heavily loaded carts creaked and rocked its way down the sleepy streets and out of Changte. In addition to the ten wagon drivers, the caravan carried eighteen mission-related people. They were Mr. and Mrs. Goforth and their four children; Nurse Chang and Fu-lin; Dr. and Mrs. Leslie and a servant; Dr. and Mrs. McKenzie, their son Douglas, and a servant; Mr. Griffith, who ran the mission school; and two women missionary-teachers.

Fu-lin sat in the last cart with Mr. Griffith and a sleepy Paul Goforth, who, though it was still too dark to read, clutched one of his illustrated adventure books as he swayed back and forth with the motion of the cart.

The first glimpse of the brassy sun over the fields and farm buildings warned of the heat that would come later in the day. Dust sparkled and danced in the narrow sunbeams that stabbed into the wagon's interior at the points where the covering quilts didn't quite meet the sides of the wagon. Fu-lin squirmed to find a more comfortable position. Unlike a lightweight rickshaw, the old heavy-wheeled wagons had no springs and jarred over rocks and ruts without mercy.

Each day seemed hotter and more miserable than the day before, and the nights provided little relief. Often the tired travelers had to camp beside the road and make do sleeping on the ground with nothing but a quilt for a bed. At the first large city they came to, they paid for a night's lodging in an inn, but they had barely settled in when a mob gathered outside demanding that the foreigners come out. When Mr. Goforth opened the door, he was pelted with dirt clods and a cry of "Kill! Kill!" from the crowd. Nothing he said would calm them down, so he ducked back in and closed the door.

"We can only pray," he said. The small group of believers began asking the Lord to protect them. At a nearby table, the cart drivers quieted their loud conversation and stopped their drinking. They watched with curiosity and murmured among themselves.

In a short time the ruckus outside the inn sub-
sided, and Fu-lin got up quietly and went to peek

through the small window. "They're gone," he said aloud, forgetting that the others were still praying. "The street's back to normal, just a few people going about their business."

"Let me see," demanded a huge driver with fat hands and fingers that looked like sausages. He marched over to the door and swung it open as though he were ready to take on the whole mob himself.

He stood at the open door for a moment and then declared, "Astounding. They are all gone!" With that, he turned around and gave Jonathan Goforth a curious look as he strode back to his table.

On Sunday afternoon, July 1, they reached the Yellow River and had to wait for the ferry to carry them across. Fu-lin was grateful to sit with Paul in the shade of a tree while the boy read one of his books out loud to Fu-lin. It seemed like none of the hardships of travel or even the threats from angry bystanders bothered young Paul. He just kept on reading.

Then suddenly, with a puzzled look on his face, he looked up at Fu-lin and said, "Why do they call you Wolf Boy?"

Fu-lin hardly knew what to say. Finally he answered, "What makes you ask that?"

Paul shrugged. "I just want to know," he said. "Is it because of your mask?"

"I suppose you could say so," said Fu-lin. Then he jumped up. "Here comes the ferry. Let's go meet it," he said, running toward the ferry landing.

At sunset, when the ferry finally delivered the missionaries to the south bank of the great river, they were excited to find some other missionaries waiting for them along with a group of foreign engineers. The engineers had come to China on a construction project they had hoped would make them rich, but now they were being chased out of China like all the other foreigners. They, however, were traveling fully armed. In addition, they had hired several soldiers on horseback to ride with them for protection.

"This must be God's provision," announced Mr. Goforth, vigorously shaking the chief engineer's hand. "There's always strength in numbers, and with your armed escort we will surely have safe passage. Praise God!"

"Not so fast," said the chief engineer. "There may be strength in numbers, but there's no speed in numbers. You would slow us down with those old mule carts. I don't know that we can agree to stay with you."

"But we have women and children," said Goforth. "You can't be thinking only of yourselves at a time like this."

"Ha!" laughed the engineer. "If I get out of this alive, a million dollars wouldn't tempt me back to this land! These people are serious, and I'm getting out no matter what."

"All the more reason why you should help us," argued Goforth.

The discussion went late into the evening, until

the engineers finally agreed to try riding with the missionaries as long as the missionaries could keep up. "But if you slow us down, that's it," said the engineers.

As the days went by, the crowds at each town seemed more and more violent. The number of people in the caravan may have been large, but the mobs grew that much larger until there were hundreds and hundreds of people at some towns. It was almost as though someone was going ahead of the caravan to announce its coming and stir up an angry crowd. "If they tried to attack us," said one of the hired soldiers, "our guns would do very little good. There are just too many people."

"Yes," the chief engineer agreed, "and if you shot someone, that would only create a bigger incident that would anger more people. Within hours, the whole countryside would hear about it, and we'd never get out of here! This is a nightmare. We've got to travel faster."

But the missionaries were far too exhausted to travel longer days. Some of them had even fallen sick, and the old carts simply couldn't go faster.

On Saturday evening, about an hour before sundown, the caravan came over a small hill to look down on the walled city of Hsintien, only a short distance away. It looked so inviting with a lazy river flowing past and lots of trees. Everyone got out of the wagons or off their horses for a brief break. "Should we camp up here or go into town?" asked Dr. McKenzie.

"Oh, I think we've got to go into town," Jonathan Goforth said. "It might be expensive, but we need a night in a decent inn where we can all get a good night's sleep and recover a little of our strength."

"Look again," said the chief engineer, who had just walked up. "A crowd is already gathering outside the gates. I don't think I'd like to stay there tonight. I doubt that there's any law in that town, but there sure enough is a mob developing. I'm for pressing on to Nanyangfu. It's a big city, and certainly the mayor will have enough soldiers to keep order and protect us. No officials want a riot on their hands."

"We can't go on to Nanyangfu," Mr. Goforth protested. "That's another nine or ten miles. The children just can't make it."

Jonathan Goforth and the other missionaries reasoned and even begged, but the engineers were determined to press on. "Tell you what I'll do," the chief engineer finally said. "We'll escort you into town and help you find an inn. Then I'll leave you one of my mounted soldiers. That'll give you some show of force. Like we said, show's the only thing of value at this point. We don't dare start shooting in a situation like this. After we've got you set up, we're moving on."

With that, a shout went up and the little caravan began to move.

Chapter 4

Saved by the Mask

THE ENGINEERS WERE BARELY OUT OF SIGHT when a crowd began to gather outside the inn where the missionaries had settled for the night. The cart drivers, who had parked their carts inside the inn's walled courtyard, pushed some of the carts against the gate as a barricade when they heard trouble developing.

"What should we do now?" asked Dr. Leslie as the missionaries and their families assembled in a small room on the second floor of the inn.

Everyone looked around at one another as though eager for some useful suggestion. While they talked, Fu-lin drifted over to the window, where he could see the yard below.

The soldier was on his horse arguing with the cart drivers, who stood around looking up at him. Soon he began gesturing toward the gate and yelling commands at them.

Hearing the ruckus outside get louder, Dr. McKenzie said, "We'd better send for help. Those engineers can't have gotten very far. Surely if we explain what's happening, they'll return to help us."

"I don't know," said Goforth. "That chief engineer was pretty stubborn."

"Yes, but they may be our only hope," said Rosalind.

"The *Lord* is our only hope," corrected Jonathan, and everyone quieted for a few moments.

"Nevertheless," said Dr. McKenzie, "it was you, Jonathan, who thought they were God's instruments to help protect us. I think we should send for them."

At that moment, Fu-lin watched the disgruntled cart drivers drag a couple of carts away from the gate and open it just enough for the soldier to spur his horse and dash out of the courtyard. Fu-lin clinched his eyes closed and groaned, *Oh no.* God might be their hope, but there went their help.

Behind him, the missionaries had agreed to send a message to the engineers. "I think that soldier is the only person we can send," said Mr. Griffith, the schoolmaster.

Fu-lin looked beyond the crowd into the growing darkness. He bet he could find the way. Wasn't his best subject geography? Wasn't he the one who had suggested this route?

"But that soldier's all the protection we have," Dr. McKenzie was saying.

"The *Lord*, Doctor, the Lord is our defender," Jonathan corrected again. "Psalm 28:7 tells us, 'The LORD is my strength and my shield; my heart trusted in him, and I am helped.' We must not forget that."

"Yes, Jonathan, you are right," conceded Dr. McKenzie.

"Please excuse me," said Fu-lin, turning back to the group, "but I don't think the soldier is going to help us. He has run away."

"What?" several people cried in unison, running to the window.

What Fu-lin said was true; the soldier was gone. Dr. McKenzie muttered something under his breath, and the others just looked at one another. What now? It would be suicide to send one of the white people out alone, and they didn't dare trust any local people. "It's going to have to be one of our own servants," Mr. Goforth said practically.

"I'll go," Fu-lin heard himself speak up.

"I didn't mean you, Fu-lin," said Mr. Goforth. "One of the men—"

"But I will go," he responded. "If you can convince one of the cart drivers to loan me a mule, I can catch the engineers. No one will pay attention to a boy on the road."

"But do you know how to ride?" asked Mr. Goforth.

"Well, yes, a little," said Fu-lin.

"We can't send him!" argued Rosalind. "What would his mother say? Besides, it's dark, and he doesn't know the way."

"Begging your pardon, honorable lady," said Fu-lin, "but there is a moon, and the road has to follow the river most of the way. I'm sure I can find them."

There was an embarrassed silence in the room as grown men and women realized that they had to rely on a fourteen-year-old boy for their help. But finally Jonathan Goforth and Fu-lin went out to beg a mule from the cart drivers.

At about midnight, Fu-lin led his mule out the inn's narrow back gate with a letter in his pocket from Mr. Goforth addressed to the chief engineer. However, following the road to Nanyangfu was not as easy as Fu-lin had imagined. There was a moon, but half the time it was behind scattered clouds, and the mule had a gait that was so rough Fu-lin nearly bounced off every time it broke into a trot. But that was rare, because Fu-lin's greatest problem was getting the animal to go faster than the slow walk it was accustomed to in pulling a cart.

It took almost two hours to cover the ten miles to Nanyangfu. As he approached the walls, he began to worry how he would ever find the engineers in such a large city in the middle of the night. It could be dangerous asking about foreigners, but who would be awake to ask?

Then, just before entering the city, his problem was solved. Outside a roadside inn, Fu-lin recognized several of the horses from the engineers' escort.

To his surprise and relief, several of the foreign engineers were hunkered over a table near the back of the inn's main room, washing down bowls of noodles with imported rum. Wordlessly he walked up to them and handed over the letter.

The chief engineer looked up at him with slightly bleary eyes. "I know you," he said. "You're from the caravan. Recognize that mask. Whatsamatter? Got a cold? Playing bandits? Heh, heh." He laughed at his little joke and opened the letter. Ignoring Fu-lin and not knowing that he could understand English, he read the letter aloud.

"Maybe we should go back and help 'em out," said one of the engineers.

"Now, wait a minute," argued the chief engineer. "You saw what just happened when we tried to enter Nanyangfu. If the mayor won't allow us in the city to stay even one night, then things are really falling apart in this country. We're not safe anywhere. I'm for getting out of China as fast as we can. At this point, it's every man for himself, I say."

A few of the other engineers argued briefly, but then they shrugged. The chief engineer scribbled a reply and handed it back to Fu-lin. They were sorry, the reply said, but they were going on immediately.

Fu-lin bowed politely and went back outside, his heart sinking. Turning the mule, he headed back to Hsintien. What would the desperate missionaries do now? As he traveled along the dark road in the wee hours of the morning, the images of his dream came back to him. Things were getting worse, just as he feared, and there seemed to be no way out.

The missionaries received the news of the uncooperative engineers with just about as much dismay as the unnamed fear growing within Fu-lin. And when the cart drivers heard that there would be no protection, they refused to leave the courtyard of the inn.

"All night long that mob has been yelling, 'Kill! Kill! Kill!' and you want us to go out that gate?" they said. "We may be nothing but humble cart drivers, but we are not *dumb* cart drivers!"

"But you are Chinese," argued Mr. Goforth. "Those people will not harm you."

"Ha!" they responded. "That's what you think. We have been helping you, the foreign white devils! Even if they don't kill us, they are likely to smash our carts just getting to you!"

Finally the missionaries wrote up a contract promising to pay for any damage to the carts or the mules or any injuries to the drivers. Only then did the cart drivers reluctantly agree to travel.

While the drivers harnessed up their mules by the dawn's pale light, the missionaries met in an empty room for prayer, and Mr. Goforth read some encouraging words from the Bible. " 'The eternal God is thy refuge, and underneath are the everlasting arms: and he shall thrust out the enemy from before thee.' 'If God be for us, who can be against us?' 'I will not fear what man shall do unto me.' "

It was time to go. When they went out to the courtyard and climbed into the carts, no one said a word. Like everyone else, Fu-lin had no idea what would be on the other side of the gate. However, as he settled down beside Paul and Mr. Griffith in the last cart, he realized that Mr. Goforth's words had eased his fears somewhat and had given him just enough faith to proceed.

The gates opened. The crowd was waiting, but it, too, was strangely quiet. As the first cart began to move forward, the crowd parted and let the missionaries pass. And then the second cart, and the third. In the last cart, Fu-lin took heart, but then he noticed that three carts ahead, Mr. Goforth was standing up and holding his baby Wallace up for the crowd to see. Wallace was laughing and cooing and waving his hands, but no one in the crowd smiled back. Something was wrong. The Chinese people loved babies, but—Fu-lin looked around—the fact that no one smiled or waved back showed that they had far more serious things on their minds.

Then he realized that even though the crowd was not screaming or throwing clods of dirt at them, there were nonetheless hateful looks on everyone's faces. Something was not right. The crowd was allowing the carts to pass, but not because the people were any less angry.

Up ahead, Fu-lin saw that the first carts of the caravan were passing through the city gates. Maybe they would get out of this city alive after all. Maybe his fears were groundless with a God who could push back the enemy like this. What had the Bible verse said again? Something like, "He shall thrust out the enemy from before thee." It was happening; they were escaping from the city.

And then, just as Fu-lin's cart passed through the gate, he saw what was before them. Both sides of the road were packed with thousands of people. In the front ranks were hundreds of Boxers with armloads of large stones or a club or spear, and here and there Fu-lin even saw a gun pointing into the air.

By this time the first carts had pulled to a stop and all the other carts had bunched up around them. A horrible cry went up from the crowd as Fu-lin's cart emerged from the gate, and a volley of stones came through the air to crash into the carts. If it had not been for the heavy layer of quilts, the stones would have smashed through the thin bamboo mats and killed the passengers.

But through the opening at the front of the cart, Fu-lin saw some of the mules go down, either hurt or killed, as stones as large as a man's fist hit them right on their heads. Somehow, Fu-lin's cart had pulled alongside Mr. and Mrs. Goforth's cart. Mr. Goforth jumped out and began yelling, "Take everything, but don't kill! Take everything, but don't kill! Take everything, but—" He didn't get the last words out of his mouth before someone hit him on the head with a stick.

Fu-lin grabbed Paul by his shirt collar and jumped to the ground, but by then the confusion was so great that it was impossible to tell in which direction safety lay. A huge Boxer waded through the brawl swinging his sword from side to side with two hands. He didn't seem to have any particular target until the broad edge of his sword struck Mr. Goforth on the side of his neck. Had it been the sharp edge, it would likely have cut off his head. Instead, it knocked the missionary to the ground with a loud grunt. Seeing that he had hit a white man, the Boxer went after him again and again. The next swing caught the brim of Mr. Goforth's pith helmet, slicing right through it but not touching his head. Goforth staggered to his feet and tried to lunge out of range before the next sword swing caught him on the back of the head, knocking him to the ground in a great cloud of dust.

Fu-lin pulled Paul away, scanning the chaos around them. For an instant his dream played across his mind and he saw himself thudding into the dust at the bottom of the cave. Now . . . the worst would happen.

Paul struggled against Fu-lin's restraining hand to go to the aid of his father. Just then another man came running up with a club as if he were going to hit Mr. Goforth, but instead he said to him, "Get away from the carts!"

Fu-lin and Paul turned and ran right into the path of a galloping horse that had lost its rider. Following its instinct not to step on a human, the horse tried to dodge to the side but in so doing lost its footing and went skidding on its side right past Fu-lin and Paul. Its head and front hooves jammed under the cart, and its back hooves, kicking madly, caught Fu-lin's ankle and tripped him to the ground. He scrambled away to avoid the flailing hooves and grabbed Paul by the collar to hurry him away.

From a short distance away they glanced back through the attack to see Mrs. Goforth standing up in her wagon, holding baby Wallace in one arm and fighting off attackers with a pillow in her other hand. Nearby, Fu-lin saw Nurse Chang carrying little Ruth Goforth and fighting with a Boxer who was trying to grab the child. Suddenly, he hit the nurse and knocked her to the ground. She covered the child with her own body to protect her. Dashing to her side, Fu-lin helped her up, then ran on with Paul in tow.

Every moment Fu-lin expected the Boxers to begin beating on him and Paul like they were on the other missionaries, but time and again the eyes of an angry person would look first at Paul and then at him and then move on. Once, a man stopped the swing of his raised club in midair when he saw that Fu-lin held Paul by the collar. He grinned at Fu-lin and hurried on to loot one of the carts.

Soon the huge crowd of onlookers began closing in and trying to loot the wagons. "No! Get out of here," yelled the Boxers. "This stuff is ours. We're the ones who are ridding China of the white devils. We deserve the spoils! Get out of here!"

Ahead of Fu-lin and Paul, a cart burst into flames. He pulled Paul to one side and kept on going, and then he looked down at the boy. Foolish Paul was still clasping an armload of his precious books.

Slowly Fu-lin realized that in the middle of this wild riot, people were stepping aside to allow him to pass. No one made any effort to stop or threaten him as he pulled Paul to safety. *Why?* he wondered as he ran ahead. Was it his mask? Did they think he was one of them, and that he was kidnapping this boy? Is that why they allowed him to pass so freely? He grinned under the cloth that hid his face. Possibly as the Wolf Boy he was saving Paul.

The two boys finally reached a place where there were fewer people. Exhausted, they stopped running and began walking through the thinning crowd. Fu-lin kept a tight grip on Paul's collar and tried to maintain a stern frown. He was glad for the mask that hid his fear and wildly beating heart.

The gravity of their situation began to sink in. Where were the rest of the missionaries? Had any survived? What about Paul's parents? Fu-lin kept walking, glancing back every few steps at the smoke and bedlam fading behind them.

What was he going to do now?

Chapter 5

The Mayor's Plot

WHEN FU-LIN AND PAUL ARRIVED at the top of a small knoll, they stopped and looked back at the scene of the attack. The smoke from the burning cart had become black and thick and obscured part of the crowd as it milled around, fighting over the loot. Among those people the boys could see, some carried boxes and chests. Some had broken into the luggage and were putting on the missionaries' clothes or waving household items like trophies. Others were fighting over some real treasures they had found.

"Hey, that's my mother's hat," yelled Paul, and he would have run back into the fray if Fu-lin had not grabbed him again.

"It doesn't matter," he said to

the boy. "She can do without her hat." He bit his lip. *If she's alive.*

And then, as they watched, the first of the other missionaries came stumbling out of the smoke and confusion. It was Dr. Leslie, almost unrecognizable for all the blood on his clothes. Fu-lin ran toward him and helped him stagger to their refuge on the knoll. He had a terrible wound on his wrist that had severed his tendons and veins when he tried to protect his head from a sword blow. It turned out that his kneecap was also severed, crippling him severely.

Then Nurse Chang came with little Ruth in her arms. Mrs. Goforth followed with baby Wallace. Paul dropped his books and ran to them, hugging his mother. One by one and two by two—sometimes leaning on each other for support—the other missionaries escaped until everyone was accounted for and standing on the knoll, except Mr. Goforth.

"I . . . I'm afraid Jonathan didn't make it," Mrs. Goforth said, holding her fist to her mouth with a frightened look on her face. "I saw him go down several times."

But then, as if by a miracle, Jonathan came crawling out of the smoke. Fu-lin and one of the other servants ran to help him get to his feet and retreat up the knoll. "We must get away from this place," he panted when he arrived. "They will soon lose interest in our belongings. Is everyone here?"

Beyond the knoll and down by the river about a half a mile away, they could see a small village, and the battered and wounded company slowly made its way there. Not knowing whether they would find friends or foes, they prayed that the Lord would open the hearts of the people to receive them. As they came near the village, men came running out waving rakes and hoes and shovels as though they were weapons. "Go away! Go away!" they yelled. "We do not want any trouble from the Boxers."

"Please," begged Mrs. Goforth as she walked right toward them in spite of their threatening behavior. "For God's sake, please help us." She pointed back at the sorry group just as Mr. Goforth fainted to the ground.

The villagers talked among themselves for a moment and then announced, "We have decided; we will help you." Just like that, they changed their minds and picked up the wounded and took the refugees into their little village. There they bathed their wounds and gave them food and drink. Dr. Leslie tried to advise them concerning how to give first aid, but he had lost so much blood that he could not get up without feeling weak.

It was only after receiving all this kindness that the missionaries discovered why the villagers finally had welcomed them. In talking with one of the people who had helped them, Jonathan Goforth discovered that the village was Moslem. Although the people did not believe in Jesus as God's Son and the Savior for all humans, they acknowledged that in some way Christians and Jews and Moslems all worshiped the same God, the God of Abraham. "Our God is your God," explained one man. "We could not face Him if we had joined in destroying you."

"Truly, God moves in mysterious ways," said Mrs. Goforth, her eyes filling with tears as she rocked little Wallace.

Whatever the villagers' reasons, Fu-lin was incredibly grateful for their hospitality. He took the bowl of stew they offered him and went outside to a secluded place behind one of the houses, where he pulled down his mask and ate hungrily. Then, exhausted, he fell asleep in the shade of the building.

Fu-lin slept for several hours. When he awoke, his muscles ached all over. Wandering stiffly back into the house where he'd left the Goforths, he saw Rosalind and the children sitting around Jonathan's bed holding his hand and praying quietly. Fu-lin's eyes widened above his mask. Mr. Goforth appeared to be dying. For a long time Fu-lin stood at the doorway, joining the family in their silent prayers.

Finally, about four o'clock in the afternoon, he heard a commotion outside the house. Going outside, he discovered five patched-together carts driving into the village. Apparently, the other carts were too damaged or their mules had been killed or the drivers had fled. Some of the five carts had wheels and other parts from the broken carts, but as it turned out, five carts were enough to carry the band of refugees now that they no longer had baggage and other household items.

Fu-lin felt a hand on his shoulder. Startled, he looked up—and there stood Mr. Goforth, looking almost like himself except for his bandages. "When I heard the rumbling of those carts, I knew that God had answered our prayer," he said in a voice that betrayed only a hint of the ordeal he had suffered. "It's a miracle! Those drivers did not have to come for us. Indeed, they are taking a great risk to help us any more at all. But God put it into their hearts to come, and here they are."

Fu-lin was transfixed. Hadn't Mr. Goforth been at death's door all afternoon? It was a miracle indeed!

Turning to the other missionaries who had gathered around, Mr. Goforth said quietly, "God has answered our prayer. It is time to press on. We must reach Nanyangfu before dark."

Into the carts the missionaries climbed, trying to make comfortable pallets from the tattered remains of the quilts for Dr. Leslie and Mr. Goforth. The missionaries tried to arrange a comfortable place for Nurse Chang as well, because, although she had not been seriously injured, she had received many bad bruises when she was protecting little Ruth from the clubs of the Boxers.

As they were leaving, some of the villagers gathered around Mrs. Goforth's cart and offered extra clothes for the children. "It may be hot during the day, but it could get chilly at night," they said. Rosalind Goforth accepted them gratefully.

Though Fu-lin knew that the jostling and bumping of the rough, old carts must be very hard on Mr. Goforth and Dr. Leslie, it was as welcome as a baby's rocking cradle to him. They were finally getting away from Hsintien. But two hours later as they approached Nanyangfu, he was not so sure that their situation had improved. For a mile along the road outside the city, people had gathered to watch their arrival. And as they got closer to the gates of the city, they could see that many more were on the tops of the walls, looking down at them.

Again, rocks and clods of dirt began to strike the carts and the mules, causing them to rear and shy. From time to time the cry of "Kill! Kill!" went up from the crowd. And yet they did not see very many Boxers, and they were able to slowly proceed even though the people pressed so close at times that it rocked the carts.

When they finally turned into the large, open yard of the inn, Fu-lin thought they would be safe, but the crowd poured in after them, preventing them from closing the gates. By the time they got out of the carts and into a room in the inn, the courtyard was packed with nearly a thousand people, pushing and yelling.

"Bring 'em out! Bring 'em out! Bring 'em out!" the crowd began to chant.

"What'll we do?" worried Mrs. McKenzie. "It's a crazed mob. We don't dare go out there."

"But if we face them and show them we are not afraid, maybe they'll calm down. I'll try speaking to them," said Mr. Goforth, struggling to his feet.

"Jonathan, you can't do that," said Mrs. Goforth. "What we need to do is get out of this city. Fu-lin said the mayor wouldn't even let the engineers enter. But possibly now that we are here, he could be persuaded to give us an armed escort out of the city. The engineers said he had soldiers. We should send for them."

"But send whom?" asked Dr. McKenzie. "That's not a crowd I'd like to try to get through alone."

"Send Fu-lin again," young Paul piped up.

"No, no. We can't ask him to go again," said Mrs. Goforth. "He's exhausted. He was on the road several hours last night and then the attack. We can't send him out again. How about one of the other servants?"

"I'm all right," spoke up Fu-lin. "I slept during the day at the village." He tugged at his mask. It had saved him before. Maybe it would make him "invisible" again.

The adults looked at one another helplessly, as though they were hoping for a better plan, but there was none. Finally Mr. Goforth said, "Thank you, Fu-lin. We greatly appreciate your offer . . . and your courage. But don't take any unnecessary chances. There's no reason to tell anyone you are associated with us. Just deliver our message as though we had hired you from off the street. Of course, we wouldn't be able to trust anyone from Nanyangfu. That's why we need you."

In a few minutes Mr. Goforth had written his message, folded it, and handed it to Fu-lin. "Let's pray for Fu-lin," he said, waving everyone to gather around.

After the prayer, Mr. Goforth said, "Fu-lin, wait until the rest of us have gone out onto the porch. Once the people see us, they won't even notice when you leave by the side door. But be careful, and . . . thank you."

Fu-lin waited. The roar from the mob increased as the missionaries filed out onto the porch. When Fu-lin could hear Mr. Goforth's clear voice trying to be heard over the noisy people, he slipped out the side door and pushed his way through the mob. The last thing he heard as he went out the gate was the missionaries trying to sing while the crowd hooted and yelled and threw things at them.

It took him some time before he found the building that housed the mayor and several of his officials. The small courtyard was dark, lit only by an oil lamp with a shade that had holes punched in it. Small beams of yellow light danced on the red door, the wall, and a low bench nearly hidden by some bushes. Fu-lin found the gong and rang it. After a long wait, an impatient clerk opened the door and took the message Fu-lin handed to him. Fu-lin waited some more, then sat down on the bench

He waited and waited. The night air was slowly cooling, and Fu-lin was getting sleepy. Mrs. Goforth had been right. He was tired, more tired than he had ever been. Finally he lay down on the bench. Folding his arm under his head as a pillow and drawing his legs up, he was just going to close his eyes . . . only for a minute, until the clerk brought out the answer. . . .

Wolf Boy slept.

He dreamed.

He tripped over a root, but instead of hitting the ground hard, the sticks and leaves gave way, and he tumbled down into a dark hole. Down, down, down he fell. His shoulder smashed into something. He flipped over and then slammed into the thick dust of the cave's floor. With his breath knocked out of him, he gasped for air and choked on a terrible, stinking odor. It smelled like urine mixed with dead animals. He coughed again. That's when he heard the low growl. The growl changed to a snarl. Before him Wolf Boy could see yellow eyes dancing back and forth . . . and then the snarl changed to a hideous laugh.

With a start, Fu-lin pulled himself up into a sitting position, his heart pounding in his ears. The yellow eyes had become beams of light from the oil lamp dancing on the uniforms of two soldiers who had just come out of the red door.

"We will get those white devils this time," the taller one said.

The shorter one laughed and shook his head. "I don't see why the mayor won't just let us go kill them in the inn."

"Of course you don't understand, because the mayor is smarter than you. That's why the mayor is the mayor, and you are just a dumb soldier. If we killed the white devils in town, then the responsibility would be on the mayor. But what if the Dowager Empress fails in her attempt to purge China of foreigners? The mayor could be charged with murder."

"Ah, I see, I see. So the mayor sends soldiers to
escort the white devils out of town like he is protect-

ing them. Meanwhile, we dress like bandits and attack them on the road. That way, if the Dowager Empress wins, the mayor can say he helped. If she loses, he can say he tried to protect the foreigners, but the bandits got them."

"Very good. Very good, honorable *dumb* soldier," said the taller man as they walked away together. "You are getting smarter."

Fu-lin sat on the bench in the shadows, breathing hard and staring at the little beams of light dancing on the wall. Wolf Boy's nightmare was coming true! He had to warn the missionaries. They did not dare trust the soldiers.

He jumped up and began running through the streets, heading back to the inn to spread the warning. Suddenly, he slowed to a walk and scratched his head. If they couldn't trust the soldiers, how would they get out of town?

Chapter 6

Wolf Boy's Escape

THE SOLDIERS ARE COMING to escort you out of the city," Fu-lin said breathlessly when he finally slipped back into the inn. He had run almost the whole way.

The missionaries sighed with relief as Fu-lin took a couple of deep breaths and a few said, "Thank God."

But Fu-lin held up both hands and shook his head. "No, no," he said. "You must not trust the soldiers. They plan to lead you into a trap!" Then he explained what he had overheard while waiting outside the mayor's house.

As he talked, he kept thinking that this was the end—the end, at least, for the white people. There seemed to be no way of escape. Either the mob outside the inn, which had not shrunk in size, would attack them, or the soldiers would lead them into an ambush on the road. One or the other. There was no escape.

This was the second night in a row that they had been trapped inside an inn with a mob outside. The night before, they had escaped from the inn only to be attacked outside the city of Hsintien. Now they seemed to face even more certain destruction if they left Nanyangfu.

While the missionaries talked together in urgent voices about what they should do, Fu-lin drifted away from the group. He opened the door a crack and peered out. The crowd was quieter now, but Fu-lin figured it was because people can keep yelling only so long. There were still a thousand or so people crammed into the courtyard, and as soon as the missionaries showed their faces, the mob would ignite again.

The smell of a sewer drifted through the door. It was a common smell in old cities where raw sewage ran down the middle of every street. But for Fu-lin it brought back visions from his dream—lying in the dust, hearing the angry snarls and snapping teeth. He knew what was coming next, and he had to get out of there.

He slammed the door and bolted it.

The missionaries were still discussing their options. "I think it would be better to face death in the open—out on the road—than to remain here," said

Dr. McKenzie. "Who knows? Maybe this plan your servant overheard will never come to pass."

"Maybe he even misunderstood," said Mrs. McKenzie hopefully.

"I doubt that," said one of the schoolteachers.

Fu-lin felt relieved that she, at least, had faith in him.

Mr. Goforth spoke up, his voice revealing the strain he was under. "I believe the boy's report is accurate, but I agree that a lot of things can happen between now and what the mayor has planned on the highway. I think we should go. But first, let's thank God for His protection. Think, my friends, how many times God has saved us already! Certainly He would not have spared our lives only to let this mob or the mayor destroy us now."

The missionary's words did not encourage Fu-lin. To him, the reassurances sounded like the hollow wishes of a dying man. Mr. Goforth was so severely wounded that he was bound to die in the next day or two anyway if he didn't get to a hospital. Fu-lin doubted that the man could continue traveling even if they were safe from mobs and "bandits."

Suddenly Fu-lin realized he'd begun thinking of the missionaries as "them" rather than "us." After all, he was not one of these white foreigners. Why should he face the same fate that awaited them? This trip was foolish. It was time he looked for an opportunity to escape.

Fu-lin had a plan in mind by the time the mayor's soldiers arrived to escort the foreigners to "safety." To be sure his plan would work, it was important that he be on the last cart—where he usually rode—but that Paul not be there with him. He could not escape if Paul was talking to him all the time or trying to show him one of his books. No, they had to be on different carts.

There were only a few soldiers, and they were foot soldiers, but somehow they managed to push the crowd back, forcing many of the people out the gate and into the street. The cart drivers hitched up their mules and lined up the wagons. Fu-lin stayed close to Paul and Mr. Griffith and urged them to get on the third wagon, but he hung back. When that cart was full, he said, "That's all right, Paul. You stay there. I'll ride in the last cart. We need some sleep now anyway. Tomorrow we can ride together and talk."

Then he hurried back to the last cart and climbed in with the wounded Dr. Leslie, his wife, and the two schoolteachers. It was a cart that had lost its arched canopy in the riot outside Hsintien. And so, to keep the hot sun off the passengers during the day, the driver had hung an old tarp over bamboo poles for an awning.

Even though it was after two o'clock in the morning, the mob was still jeering and chanting, "Kill! Kill!" But the soldiers kept them back so that the carts could move out of the inn's courtyard and down the street. Soon they arrived at the city gate. Fu-lin could see that hundreds of people had climbed to the top of the wall. Many of them held torches, and Fu-lin was certain that it was only the presence of the soldiers that prevented them from throwing their torches or stones or other items down on the carts as they passed through the gates.

Outside the city gates the mob thinned, but there were still too many people along the roadway for Fu-lin to drop from his cart unnoticed and make an escape. As they slowly rolled away from Nanyangfu, he looked back at the city. A slight glow lit the dark sky above the city and silhouetted the people standing on the wall, some of them still holding their torches. But just above the gate, Fu-lin noticed a different kind of light. It was unusually bright, possibly created by a lamp with a reflector, but it also was flashing, shining out long and short bursts. Fu-lin frowned. It was a code. Someone was sending a signal, and he knew exactly what it meant. The message announced to the "bandits" that the caravan of foreigners was on its way.

Fu-lin looked around. It was time to escape! They were away from the city now, and bystanders no longer lined the road. Dr. and Mrs. Leslie appeared to have fallen asleep, and the two schoolteachers were huddled near the front of the cart peering past the driver at the dim road ahead. Fu-lin peeked under the edges of the quilts on both sides. There were no soldiers walking beside his cart. Possibly they had gone ahead and hitched a ride on another cart. This was his chance.

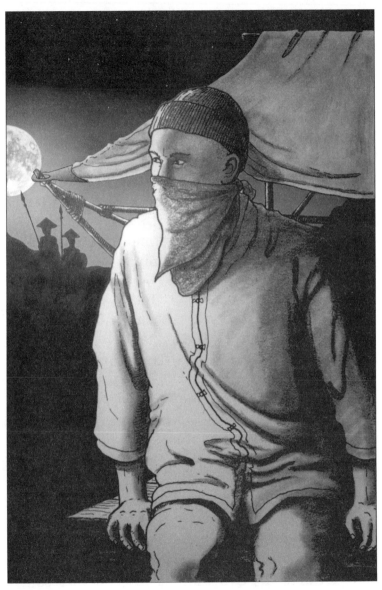

Fu-lin was just slipping out the back of his cart,
confident that no one would notice his departure,

when the loud cry of a woman's voice came from somewhere ahead. "Stop! Stop the wagon train!" And all the carts came to a stop. The cry was so frantic that Fu-lin had no idea who was screaming until the woman began calling, "Paul! Paul! Paul! Where are you?" It was Mrs. Goforth.

Soon her husband's voice joined hers, and then other people began taking up the cry. "Paul! Mr. Griffith! Paul! Where are you?"

Fu-lin dropped to the ground. He couldn't slip away unnoticed now, not with everyone milling around. Stifling his disappointment, he walked up the line to see what was happening.

When he got to the front of the caravan, Mr. Goforth had both hands on the shoulders of the driver of the third cart. "Tell us again. Exactly what happened?" he demanded.

Throwing his hands up in a gesture of helplessness, the driver explained, "I was just driving along when I looked around, and they were gone."

"When did you notice this?" demanded Mrs. Goforth.

"Just a few minutes ago. I'm hired to drive the cart, not baby-sit your son. How should I know when he jumped out?"

"Then they can't be far," said Mr. Goforth. "We will search for them."

One hour, then two went by as people searched for Paul and Mr. Griffith, but with no success. At first the soldiers grumbled and begged them to proceed, but Mrs. Goforth would not hear of it. "He is my son," she said indignantly. "He cannot have disappeared into thin air. I will not leave until every possible place has been searched."

Finally the soldiers gave up and climbed into the carts to rest.

Fu-lin walked with Mr. and Mrs. Goforth back toward the city until they met some people who were still by the road. "Have you seen a white man and a little boy on foot?" Mr. Goforth asked.

The people looked at one another, and Fu-lin thought he saw a hint of a smile cross the man's face before he spoke up. "Oh yes," he said. "They came running back this way shortly after your carts passed us. The man was crazy. He threw the boy in that well over there and then jumped in after him."

"Oh my goodness," cried Mrs. Goforth in a feeble voice. "How can that be?"

"Now, Rosalind," said Jonathan in a not-too-certain tone of voice, "you know Mr. Griffith would never do such a thing."

"But these have been terrible times for all of us. Who knows what he might have done?" She turned to the other people and said, "Did any of the rest of you see this?"

"Oh yes, oh yes," they said, nodding their heads vigorously.

"Then we must search the well," she said.

The Goforths called again and again into the well, but there was no answer. It was only after Mr. Goforth promised to pay the onlookers a considerable sum of money that they agreed to get ropes and a lantern for searching the well. But it took them a half hour before they returned with the equipment, and by then several other people from the caravan had arrived. The local people handed over the ropes and lantern, collected their money, and walked away.

After some discussion, Dr. McKenzie volunteered to go down into the well, but it took ever so long to arrange the ropes so he could be lowered down into the well with the small lantern.

"Hurry," pleaded Rosalind Goforth. "Every minute counts if they are hanging on to the wall."

One of the drivers cruelly pointed out, "If they were hanging on to the wall, they could have answered us when we called down to them."

For a moment Mrs. Goforth burst into tears, but then she got ahold of herself.

Fifteen minutes later, Dr. McKenzie called up from the bottom of the well. "There's no one down here," he yelled. "The water is only two feet deep, and the only thing in it is an old waterlogged bucket. Pull me up."

When the travelers were all standing on the road again, Mr. Goforth said, "We've done all we can, Rosalind. We've looked everywhere. All we can do is entrust Paul—and Mr. Griffith—into God's hands and go on."

His wife nodded. "At least we know they aren't drowned in the bottom of the well," she said in a small voice. The tired, frightened, and discouraged little company walked back to their carts. When they arrived, they found that the soldiers had climbed into their carts and fallen asleep.

"Now what are we going to do?" said Mrs. McKenzie.

"Wake them up, of course," said Dr. McKenzie. "They didn't pay to ride; besides, we all know that they are leading us into a trap."

Mr. Goforth stepped forward and held a finger to his lips. "No. Don't awaken them," he whispered. "We'll just double up. We can make it."

In that decision, Fu-lin saw his chance. He hung back, and when the carts were as full as they could be, he said from behind his mask, "I'll walk for a while, and then trade off with someone."

He walked along behind the last cart until they had gone a mile or so and everything had quieted down. Then he just stopped in the dark. As the carts lumbered ahead, he edged off the road and slipped behind a tree. Good. He had escaped whatever awaited the missionaries down the road.

Wolf Boy was no longer one of them!

Chapter 7

Rescue of the Bible Woman

MILE AFTER WEARY MILE PASSED as Fu-lin trudged toward home in the dark, past Nanyangfu, past the little Moslem village, and past Hsintien. The sun was just coming up when he arrived at the top of the hill above Hsintien where the missionaries and engineers had first looked down on the city.

It had been in Hsintien that serious trouble really started for the missionaries. Before then on their trip south, they had faced several angry groups of people throwing clods of dirt and yelling threats, but outside Hsintien they had nearly lost their lives.

 Fu-lin dropped down under a gnarled oak tree, so exhausted he could hardly move. With his elbows on his knees, he cupped

his chin in his hands. By now the missionaries would certainly be dead. The soldiers had probably led them into the ambush before dawn. He cringed at the thought of little Ruth and the other children being killed. They didn't deserve such a terrible end, but what could *he* have done? He was lucky to have escaped with his own life.

And what had happened to Paul and Mr. Griffith? They'd probably gotten out of the cart so Paul could relieve himself. Caught away from the safety of the caravan, they'd probably been dragged away by the angry townspeople—maybe even the ones who tried to pretend that they'd jumped into the well. Tears welled in Fu-lin's eyes. Paul had looked up to him—and now he was dead.

Mr. and Mrs. Goforth had been good to him and didn't deserve death, and the schoolteachers had taught him so much. His shoulders shook with soundless sobs. Why had this happened? Wasn't their God big enough to protect them? Mr. Goforth had always said He was. And the missionaries had been serving Him, preaching the Gospel, and telling people about Jesus.

Fu-lin had heard that message, and he had believed. But on this trip doubt had crept into his mind. Throughout the trip they had prayed so hard for God's protection. They had counted it as God's protection when they had escaped with their lives from the attack at Hsintien, hardly even noticing that He had not protected their possessions. They had lost everything they owned. If God was so powerful, why hadn't He protected them completely?

Fu-lin looked down the river where he could just see some thin threads of smoke rising above the trees. It probably came from the cooking fires of the Moslem village. Those people weren't even Christians, so how could God have been behind their kindness? At the time, Fu-lin also had believed that God had saved them, but now . . . now the missionaries were surely dead, and he felt alone and lost. What good was a God who let His servants die? Who even let innocent little children die?

In his exhaustion, he fell asleep.

Wolf Boy dreamed. He tripped over a root and was falling. But what looked like solid ground proved to be a cave entrance covered by sticks and leaves. He fell through the hole and tumbled down into a dark cavern. Down, down he fell. His whole body jerked in readiness to slam into the dusty floor of the cave. . . .

But he did not hit the bottom. Instead, he awoke with bright light stabbing his eyes. His heart hammered to escape his chest. Air—he couldn't gulp enough. Sweat dripped off of him.

He squinted through the bright sunlight and then released his breath in a burst, making his mask flap. He was sitting under the oak tree by the road above Hsintien—right where he had fallen asleep early that morning. Slowly his heart and breathing returned to normal. He cocked his head to the side and frowned. His dream had changed. It had not ended with the awful smell and the feeling that something worse was about to happen. What could that mean? Maybe . . . maybe it changed because the worst had already happened! The missionaries were probably all dead. His schooling had ended, and God—if He existed at all—did not answer prayer.

Fu-lin arose and kept walking slowly toward Changte, kicking stones ahead of him from time to time. If he had nothing else to fear, it was because the worst had already happened. Far from feeling relieved, he felt defeated, like the world had ended but he had survived—left behind, alone, to face all the consequences. He had no food and no money, but he didn't care. What difference did it make? He was walking toward Changte only because there was no place else to go. His mother and sister and brothers were there, and they would be glad to see him, glad that he was safe, but suddenly he realized that there was more to life than just surviving. While living with the Goforths, he had lived with a purpose, a direction—but now that had vanished.

An argument began to take place in his mind: Yes, he had saved himself, but had he abandoned the missionaries? On the other hand, there was nothing he could have done to help them—or was there? They knew that they were heading right into a trap. In fact, he'd tried to warn them! So it wasn't his fault.

Yet the more he went over the events of the night before, the worse he felt. He felt like a failure.

On the trip south, Fu-lin and Paul had often hopped off their cart. It had seemed easy to walk faster than the old mules then, but now he realized that they had only walked a short time, an hour or two at the most. It was much harder to walk that fast all day. From dawn to dark the old mules could keep going until their lumbering pace had covered twenty-five miles or so per day. But on his way back to Changte, Fu-lin found himself exhausted before noon. Twenty-five miles was an incredible distance for a boy to walk, and doing it day after day was almost impossible, especially when he had to also beg for food or find scraps in garbage piles.

When he finally got to the Yellow River—without money to pay the ferry—he wasted half a day trying to find a fisherman who would take him across in a boat. He found no one, but finally someone told him about a place downriver where he could wade across if he used a pole to carefully test the river bottom and help him keep his balance. Getting there and making the crossing took the rest of the day.

The caravan had traveled south from Changte to Nanyangfu in twelve days, but it took Fu-lin twenty days to get home.

Darkness was descending on Sunday evening, July 29, when Fu-lin staggered into Changte. There was a terrible smell of smoke in the air, and people were scurrying around, sneaking here and there, not speaking to one another on the streets.

Fu-lin had intended to go straight home, but the Chou family home was on the other side of the city, and to get there he had to walk right past the mission compound. He would just take a look around for old times' sake. But as he approached the low walls, something seemed different. The thatched roof over the charcoal shed that usually could be seen over the wall was just a skeleton silhouetted against the evening's purple sky. What had happened? He cautiously approached the gate, the smell of smoke getting stronger with every step. He knocked, but his knock alone caused the gate to swing open. It had not been locked.

He stood, dazed, at the ruined compound before him. The main house was still standing—though without a window—but the charcoal shed had been burned. And the fire had been recent. Smoke still curled from a pile of rubble, and small flames still licked at a beam leaning against the outside garden wall.

In shock, Fu-lin walked around the courtyard, tripping over things that had been torn out of the house and thrown into the yard. He had spent so many good times in this pleasant home. Now it had been ransacked, vandalized. Fu-lin felt sick. Not only had the missionaries all died, but their very memory had been destroyed!

Just then a faint moaning sound drew his attention toward the old tree by the charcoal shed. Moving closer, he shook himself out of his daze. What was making that sound? He was into the deep shadows under the tree before he realized that a long, dark object hung from a large limb. Ever so slightly, it

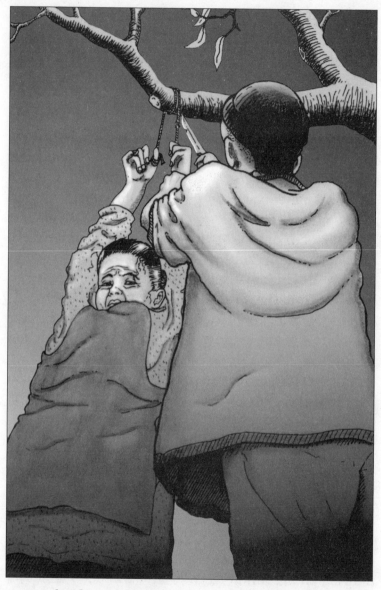

swung back and forth. "Oh . . . oh . . . oh." The feeble
groans sounded in time with the motion, like a slow

grandfather clock that moaned instead of ticked. "Oh . . . oh . . . oh."

"Ahh!" screamed Fu-lin as he jumped back. "It's a body!"

"Help . . . help me," a weak voice wailed.

"W-who. . . ?" stammered Fu-lin. "Mrs. Chang? Is that you?"

Cautiously, Fu-lin reached out to touch the slowly swinging object. It was indeed Mrs. Chang, the old Bible woman. She was hanging from the tree by thin cords tied to her thumbs!

Quickly Fu-lin hunted around until he found the old buckets in which he had carried water from the fountain and a dull knife sometimes used for cutting weeds in the yard. He turned one bucket upside down below Mrs. Chang. It was just high enough for the old woman to stand on and take the weight off her thumbs. Fu-lin stood on the other bucket and, reaching as high as he could, cut the cords. Could she live? Would she ever be able to use her injured thumbs again?

The old woman was so weak that the moment Fu-lin released her, she fell to the ground. "I'm sorry," he mumbled, crouching beside her and helping her to sit up. "I meant to catch you. What . . . what has happened? Why were you hanging here?"

The pain in the old woman's thumbs and arms must have been dreadful, but she fixed terrified eyes on Fu-lin's face. "Boxers," she said weakly, her lips trembling. "They raided our church service this morning." After taking several deep breaths to calm herself, she clutched his shirt. "Wolf Boy—you must find Mr. Ho. They . . . have taken him away. We must not let them kill our elder."

Fu-lin shook his head. He wanted to stay and help the Bible woman, but she insisted. "I am old and ready to meet my Jesus . . . but the church needs Mr. Ho. It is much more important that you find and help him. Now go!" she urged.

Staring wide-eyed at her as though he could not believe what he was seeing, Fu-lin backed away toward the gate. When he bumped into it, he turned and fled down the street. He ran past other burned buildings—some of them with broken furniture and personal belongings strewn in the streets outside. Some of the homes he recognized as belonging to some of the other believers.

Where would the Boxers have taken Mr. Ho? The Boxers had the blessing of the government; they didn't have to hide. If they wanted to make an example of him, they would probably take the church elder to a public place. . . .

Fu-lin headed for the marketplace.

His guess was correct. A noisy crowd filled the street in front of the local courthouse. Fu-lin pushed his way through the jostling bodies until he could see Mr. Ho standing on the courthouse steps. Fu-lin flinched. The gentle man had been beaten. His clothes were torn, one eye was swollen nearly closed, and blood trickled from a wound over his left ear.

The court magistrate stood before Mr. Ho, holding his hands up for silence from the crowd. "Why have you brought this man to me?" he demanded of the crowd.

Laughs and jeers went up on every side, and then a man yelled, "The foreign devils have fled, and their dupe, devil number two, is in a fix. Kill him! Cut him in quarters as a warning to all the other dupes."

"Yes, kill him! Quarter him!" echoed the crowd.

"Why have you become a follower of these foreign devils?" the magistrate demanded. "What can you hope to gain? You disgrace yourself and your country."

"Your Honor," replied Mr. Ho with a slight bow, "I am not following foreigners. I am following the living and true God. The gods that I used to worship were not gods at all. By profession, I was an idol maker. I made them with these hands," he said, holding up his hands.

With a slight smile, he said to the magistrate, "You, sir, should be glad I have found the true God, because I used to break every law in this city and was often brought into your court. But ever since I became a Jesus follower, I have not once been arrested and have broken no laws."

The surprised official grabbed Mr. Ho by both shoulders and looked him in the eyes. "Yes," he said, "I do remember you now. You were one of the worst troublemakers in this city, but I haven't heard of any problems from you for a long time. What do you do now?"

"I am an elder in our church," Mr. Ho said boldly. "In addition, I have started a restaurant. It is a little different than most. People don't sit down to eat. My family and I cook the food and deliver it to whoever wants it."

"Ah!" said the magistrate. "I have heard of you. It is said that your food is very good and the prices are fair. Huh. It would make my job a whole lot easier if all the thieves and troublemakers in this city took a lesson from you."

The magistrate turned to the mob of people in the street. "All you people go home now!" he ordered. "This man hasn't done anything wrong, and I intend to protect him as an upright citizen of our fair city. Let it be a warning to the rest of you: If anyone lays a hand on him, they'll answer to me. Do you understand? Now, go home."

Fu-lin was astonished. This magistrate was known to be very harsh, and it would not have surprised him if Mr. Ho had been condemned to death. But instead, Mr. Ho had received his support and protection!

Fu-lin hung back as the people dispersed, some of them grumbling and shaking their heads. Once Mr. Ho and the magistrate had exchanged bows, Fu-lin followed Mr. Ho down the street.

"Mr. Ho," he called when they were away from the crowd.

The surprised elder turned around with a start at seeing the masked youth, possibly fearing another attack.

"It's just me, Fu-lin, Mr. Ho. I have returned. I found Mrs. Chang alive at the mission, but . . . it has been burned and vandalized."

The next thing Fu-lin knew, Mr. Ho had enveloped him in a warm hug. "What about Mr. and Mrs. Goforth?" the wounded elder asked eagerly. "Did they escape? Are they all right?"

Fu-lin hung his head. "I am sad to report, honorable elder, that . . . they have all been killed." Taking the man's arm to steady him, the masked boy walked the battered and bruised Mr. Ho toward his home as he told the sad story of their journey.

Chapter 8

Back From the Dead

O<small>N</small> A<small>UGUST</small> 14, 1900, a combined column of thousands of British, French, Japanese, Russian, German, and American troops marched into Peking and occupied the capital city. Many foreign warships had situated themselves in Chinese ports with their huge guns trained on the surrounding cities. Up until this point the Chinese government had ignored or—in the case of the Dowager Empress—had encouraged the Boxer Rebellion. The occupation of their ports and capital city by foreign troops further humiliated and enraged the Chinese people, and the Boxer Rebellion gained momentum until between two and three hundred missionaries, as well as many other foreigners, had been killed.

During this terrible summer, the Changte Christians continued to meet secretly in one another's homes, but Fu-lin did not join them. He lived with his mother and siblings and avoided the Christians whenever he could. His depression was overwhelming. Sometimes it troubled him that he had deserted the missionaries, but he tried to comfort himself with the argument that he had no choice. They had been killed, and he would be dead as well if he had remained with them.

At least he wasn't having the dream anymore.

To keep busy and help his mother, Fu-lin did odd jobs and ran errands for the local druggist. It was a good job, even though people sometimes looked oddly at the mask he wore. By the time a year had passed, the druggist had entrusted him to deliver medicines to the homes of his customers.

On September 7, 1901, news spread through the streets of Changte that the Chinese government had signed a peace treaty agreeing to put down the Boxers and pay huge fees to all the foreign groups that had suffered damage. At last! The Boxer Rebellion was officially over—but not the anger of the Chinese people, Fu-lin noticed as he trotted through the streets on his errands. They did not welcome the return of foreigners or their ideas, including their Christian religion.

One day as Fu-lin picked up the medicines he was supposed to deliver, he was startled to see that a delivery of medicine for typhoid fever was addressed to the old mission compound. Fu-lin did not know anyone lived there. But as he approached the old compound, he could see that someone had repaired the place and painted the door. The man who answered his knock was a thin, sickly-looking white man suffering—undoubtedly—from typhoid.

"I have your medicine for you, honorable sir," Fu-lin said in English, hoping that might earn him a larger tip.

Through pale, watery eyes the man stared at him and then said in a thin voice, "That mask . . . is that you, Chou Fu-lin?" The bony man stepped forward, holding on to the doorframe with one hand and reaching out with the other. "You've grown up. How . . . how are you, boy?"

Fu-lin was so surprised that a foreigner would know his name that he turned and ran from the house.

"Fu-lin, come back!" called the man. "You know me—Jonathan Goforth. Please come back!"

Fu-lin stopped and stared at the frail man swaying unsteadily in the doorway. How could that be? The man had some resemblance to Mr. Goforth. But Mr. Goforth had been killed over a year and a half ago! Unless he was seeing a ghost, this couldn't be him!

The man was thin and white enough to be a ghost, but the more he stared, Fu-lin could see that there was *some* substance to him. He could not see through him. Slowly he approached the man in the doorway. Could it be—?

"I'm so glad to see you!" said Mr. Goforth, managing a weak smile. "We had no idea what happened to you after that dreadful night outside of Nanyangfu. Some thought the Boxers had grabbed you. Others said . . . well, we just didn't know. But here you are, safe and sound. God be praised!"

It was Mr. Goforth. There was no doubt.

"And I . . . I thought you were dead," Fu-lin stammered. "Your honorable wife, and the children?" He hesitated, afraid to ask. "Are . . . are they alive, too?"

"Oh yes. They are quite well—better than I am, I pray. But they aren't here," he added quickly when Fu-lin tried to peer past him into the house. "I'm alone for now. The family will be along later—as soon as possible. As soon as I heard the Boxer Rebellion was over, I left Canada to come back and get the mission work started again. But as you can see, I've been ill. . . ." Mr. Goforth stroked his bearded chin below his sunken cheekbones. "Which reminds me, Fu-lin, I could use some help. I'm slowly getting better, but . . . well, would you be interested in working for me again?"

The mask covered Fu-lin's astonishment. He hardly knew what to say. Of course he would like to work for the Goforths again, but . . . would they want him when they learned that he had deserted them? Fu-lin dropped his eyes and scuffed his sandal in the dirt. Mr. Goforth probably already knew. The other Christians certainly would have told him how he had come back saying that everyone was dead. On the other hand—Fu-lin looked down the street and scratched his head—he hadn't told anyone *exactly* when and how he had left the missionaries. Maybe Mr. Goforth didn't know and wouldn't have to find out.

"Yes, honorable sir," he said humbly. "If you will have me, I will tell my mother tonight. I'm sure she will approve."

Excited, Fu-lin ran to finish his other deliveries. Only one thought bothered him: Would Mr. Goforth insist on knowing how he'd disappeared outside Nanyangfu?

Fu-lin was happy to be working for Mr. Goforth again. He scrubbed floors, carried water, built the charcoal fires, ran errands, and even did some cooking. One day as he was serving Mr. Goforth a rather watery soup of noodles and vegetables, the missionary looked up from a letter he was reading from his wife. "Well," Mr. Goforth said to Fu-lin, "it looks like you won't be seeing Paul until vacation time."

Fu-lin's eyes opened wide with surprise. If he hadn't been wearing his mask, Mr. Goforth would have seen his mouth drop open, as well.

"What's so unusual about that?" said Mr. Goforth. He held up the letter and shook it slightly. "Rosalind says right here that she's going to leave Paul and Helen at the China Inland Mission School in Chefoo. But don't worry. On holidays they'll come home, and then you'll get to see him."

"But I didn't know that he was . . . was . . ." stammered Fu-lin. "That you found him." In fact, he had wondered how the missionaries had escaped, but he'd been afraid to ask for fear of having to admit that he had abandoned the caravan.

"Oh, of course," said Mr. Goforth, smiling and taking a deep breath. "You wouldn't know anything about what happened after we left Nanyangfu, would you?" The missionary's health was returning, and his steely blue eyes seemed to look straight through Fu-lin.

"No, sir," said Fu-lin.

"And so you might think Paul was dead . . . even though I've returned. Right?"

"Right. He was missing when we . . . when you finally left." Fu-lin glanced toward the back door. Maybe it was time to go fetch some water from the neighborhood fountain. He was curious, but if he stayed to listen, would he be expected to tell what he had done that night? They really were running low on water.

"Well, it was the most remarkable act of God that I've ever witnessed. Sit down, young man, and I'll tell you," said Jonathan with a wide sweep of his hand toward a stool. "You were there, weren't you, when we were looking for Paul and Mr. Griffith . . . in the well, and all of that?"

Fu-lin cleared his throat and swallowed. "Yes, sir."

"Well, we couldn't find them anywhere, and by the time we got back to the caravan, the soldiers had fallen asleep in our wagons. Some of the folks wanted to wake them up and make them walk, but something—I believe it was the Holy Spirit—told me to let them sleep, so we all piled in as well as we could. We traveled on for about half an hour until we came to a fork in the road. In the dark, none of us knew which was the correct path, so the first driver let his mule have its head, and all the rest followed.

"The eastern sky was just starting to lighten when the soldiers woke up. And were they furious! According to them, we had taken the wrong road. But by then a couple of our drivers recognized the road we were on. It was a bit out of the way but still heading where we wanted to go.

"You see, there were two roads: one with the ambush, the other safe but slightly longer. God had caused the soldiers to fall asleep and guided our mules to take the safe road. The soldiers couldn't do anything but grumble and complain and walk back to Nanyangfu."

Fu-lin stared at Mr. Goforth. If the man weren't sitting right before him, he would have had a hard time believing the story. But obviously God *had* saved them, just as they had prayed. Fu-lin placed his palm against his forehead and ran his fingers through his hair. Then he adjusted his mask a little higher. What did this mean? His dreams had done nothing but frighten him into acting the coward! How could he ever live that down?

"Oh yes, about Paul . . ." continued Mr. Goforth. He moved his head to the side to catch Fu-lin's line of sight, which at that moment was staring at nothing. "Are you with me, son?" When Fu-lin blinked and focused back on him, he continued. "It seems that Mr. Griffith was so concerned about this ambush we were facing, that when he saw a chance to escape, he grabbed Paul and just ran for it. They got lost, however, and wandered around who-knows-where. A couple of days later, a letter caught up to us saying that Mr. Griffith and Paul had been found and were safe. We sent an escort to get them and were reunited by midnight.

"So you see," he said, leaning back in his chair, "God was with us all the way. In fact, if you think about it, God used that delay of our searching for Mr. Griffith and Paul to protect the rest of us. If we hadn't been stopped there all that time, the soldiers wouldn't have fallen asleep."

Without thinking Fu-lin blurted, "Were there any more mobs?"

"Oh yes," said Jonathan with a nod. "We faced more mobs and more violence, but God saw us through, and everyone's life was spared. We even joined up with the engineers again when we got to Fancheng. They couldn't believe we were still alive, either.

"After that, we traveled ten days by houseboat down to Hankow, and then we boarded a steamer for Shanghai and, of course, sailed from there to Canada."

Fu-lin's mind was spinning. Without saying thank you or excuse me, he slipped down off the stool and went out the back door, where he picked up the water buckets and headed for the fountain, shaking his head as he walked. God had saved the missionaries! God had even used Mr. Griffith's efforts to save Paul by running, but what did that mean for Fu-lin? He, too, had run . . . but it was to save his own skin, doubting God more and more with every step toward home.

He had missed the victory because he had fled the battle.

Chapter 9

The Dream's Meaning

FU-LIN SNIFFED. Something was burning! He ran in from the backyard, where he had been hanging out some laundry to dry. Not again! The rice was scorching. It seemed like he never could cook it right. Either he didn't start with enough water or the fire was too hot or he forgot about it—like this time—but one way or another, he wasn't a very good cook.

Until Mrs. Goforth and the children arrived, there was no need for more than one helper in the house. Fu-lin shook his head. If he didn't learn how to cook better—and soon—he might lose his job. Nurse Chang, who had recently returned from Shanghai, where she had worked for a year, had already offered to help.

He quickly scooped out the top, unburned portion of the rice and put it in two bowls. Then he poured the vegetable and fish stew over it and carried one of the bowls in to the table, where Mr. Goforth was working.

"Thank you," the missionary said absentmindedly. Then he looked up at Fu-lin. "Why don't you come in here and eat with me tonight? I need some company, and it feels like you are nothing but a servant when you always eat alone in the kitchen. I'd rather we be friends."

Unconsciously, Fu-lin put his hand to his mask.

"Ah," said Jonathan Goforth with a wave, "don't worry about that. I'm the only one who'll see you, and I saw what you looked like long ago when your parents first brought you here. It's not going to bother me."

Fu-lin could feel a wave of heat rising up his chest into his neck, and he was sure his face was blushing. What he looked like still bothered him— almost frightened him if he caught a glimpse of himself in a mirror without his mask. It was nice of Mr. Goforth to invite him, but he couldn't imagine that it wouldn't bother him, too.

"Besides," urged Mr. Goforth, "there's something I want to talk to you about."

Fu-lin caught a whiff of the dinner that he had prepared for Mr. Goforth. It still emitted a scorched smell. Oh no! Here it came: Mr. Goforth was going to tell him to find another job. He shrugged. What difference did it make if Mr. Goforth saw him without his mask? It was all over anyway.

Fu-lin went to the kitchen and returned with his bowl and sat down on the other side of the table. Slowly he pulled his mask down and let it hang around his neck like a bandana.

"Let's thank God for our food," said Mr. Goforth.

Fu-lin watched the missionary bow his head and close his eyes as he thanked the Lord for their food. Fu-lin frowned. Closing his eyes—that was a neat way for Mr. Goforth to avoid looking at him.

But the moment the prayer was over, the missionary looked up directly at Fu-lin and smiled. "Well, shall we begin?" After a couple of bites, Mr. Goforth added, "What I want to ask you about is, what happened to you that night when we got separated? Do you mind telling me?"

Fu-lin put his left hand over his face, but the older man was not gazing at his face. It was as if . . . as if he was looking into his heart. "I . . . I," stammered Fu-lin. He hadn't been expecting this. He could say that he had gone back to make one more search for Paul and missed the caravan leaving—but no. He wasn't going to add lying to his list of offenses. He swallowed and looked down at his bowl. "Well, you see, I was sure you were all going to be killed, and I didn't know what I could do to help, so I . . ." His voice trailed off.

"What made you so sure we were going to be killed?" prodded Mr. Goforth.

"I warned you what I heard the soldiers saying outside the mayor's house."

"Oh yes," said Mr. Goforth, "and we believed you. We even saw a signal light sending a message from the top of the wall. But, son, don't you see? God has a purpose for us, and until that purpose is accomplished, nothing can harm us as long as we are obeying Him. How else could we have escaped the mob at Hsintien or get out of Nanyangfu?"

"Yes, I know," said Fu-lin, looking down at his bowl again. It truly was remarkable how they had escaped all those times—but there also had been his dream. He had been so certain. Finally he looked up. "I had this dream. . . . I often have it—or I used to. It's always the same." He stopped and covered his face with his hand again. "It's about how I became the Wolf Boy. In the dream I am falling down into the cave, and it feels like something terrible is about to happen. But I always wake up just before it happens. It's like telling the future. Every time I had the dream, it came true. Something worse did happen. The dream came again, just before I overheard the soldiers tell about the mayor's plot. I was sure it meant you were going to die."

"What do you mean, every time you had this dream, it came true? Give me an example," said Mr. Goforth.

Fu-lin frowned, then brightened. "Well, the night before we buried Florence, I had the dream, then that afternoon we heard about the Boxers stopping the mail, and two days later we got the instructions to leave Changte. So you see, the dream foretold the Boxer Rebellion."

Mr. Goforth put down his bowl and chopsticks and leaned back in his chair. He clasped his hands together on the top of his head with his fingers laced together. After a moment he said, "It's true that God spoke to people in the Bible through dreams, sometimes warning them of danger or giving direction for the future. But God never turned anyone into a fortune-teller by giving the person a recurring dream to show whether one day would be good and another bad. God doesn't want us to become superstitious or fearful. We have to build our understanding of truth and how God speaks to us in His Word, the Bible. Everybody dreams, and a lot of things cause our dreams—things that have happened to us during the day, fears or hopes we have for the future, frightening experiences from our past." A wry grin spread across his face, and his eyes twinkled in the lamplight as he glanced down at his bowl of fish stew and scorched rice. "Maybe even something we've eaten that disagrees with our stomach can bring on an unsettling dream," he added with a chuckle.

Then he took his hands off his head, leaned forward with one arm on the table, and pointed gently at Fu-lin with his other hand. "You said your dream is very similar every time. That sounds to me like it comes more from that experience in your past than a message from God."

"But—how can I be sure?" said Fu-lin.

Jonathan Goforth leaned back again. "Well, I

can't say for sure where your dream came from. Possibly just left over from your past. But I am sure that it did not come from the Lord. Why? Because it didn't come true! You expected the worst—that we would all be killed—and that didn't happen, so it couldn't have been a message from the Lord. Any word from the Lord will always prove trustworthy and true."

Fu-lin just stared at the missionary. He still hadn't told Mr. Goforth exactly what he'd done that night. But if what Mr. Goforth said about his dream was true, then he'd been nothing more than the worst kind of coward.

On the evening that Mrs. Goforth and the three younger children arrived that spring, Nurse Chang returned to help. What a celebration it was! Fu-lin was very grateful that he did not have to do all the cooking, even though he had finally learned how to cook rice without burning it.

As Fu-lin was cleaning up the table, Mr. Goforth turned eagerly to his wife, who had just come back into the room after settling the children in the adjoining room on the hard kang sleeping platform. "Rosalind," he said, "won't you come and sit down. I've got so much to tell you—plans about the future. I can hardly wait."

She gracefully sat across from him at the table and reached across to take his hand.

"It's almost unbelievable," he said, "but the mission board has assigned me the whole region north of Changte. Can you imagine that? And God has given me a plan for developing it."

"That's wonderful, Jonathan. What is it?"

"Rosalind, when I realized that God saved us when so many other missionaries lost their lives in the Boxer Rebellion, I began to understand how important was the work that He has for us to do. As I studied the Scripture and how the early church spread, I realized that nothing is more important in missionary work than evangelism and planting churches—nothing! Education, medical work, everything else is secondary. So I needed a plan, a new method that would focus on evangelism and church planting."

Mrs. Goforth looked at him eagerly. "Continue, Jonathan. I can tell by the twinkle in your eye that God has not left you 'planless.'"

"Well, no. Of course He hasn't. You see, we will travel from town to town, renting a building in each town for a month. You can live there and preach to the women during the day while I go out with a team to evangelize the surrounding area. Each night we'll have a meeting back in our building."

As a startled look appeared on Mrs. Goforth's face, Jonathan stopped for a moment and then continued. "Oh, Rosalind, don't worry. You can play the organ, and we'll sing plenty of gospel hymns. It'll be great, and at the end of a month, we'll leave an evangelist there and move on to a new town."

Fu-lin gathered up the remaining dishes and moved away from the table. The Goforths were planning to leave? What about him? Maybe they didn't want him around anymore. This would be a good excuse to leave him behind. He couldn't blame them. Mr. Goforth had not pressed him on his story of exactly what happened that night in Nanyangfu, but it wasn't too hard to figure out that he'd run away because he'd been afraid.

"But, Jonathan!" Mrs. Goforth cried. "What about the children? We can't drag them all over the country with no chance to make a decent home. Think of how long it takes to set up a decent home in this country. Why, you've been here for months, and it's still a mess."

Her husband laughed uncomfortably. "That's because Fu-lin and I have been living like a couple of bachelors. It won't take any time for you to bring some grace and charm back to it. But don't worry, dear. This will always be our real home, and we'll even live here part of the year."

"But—what about the Boxers? Officially, they may be subdued, but in the small towns, there are bound to be people who still hate foreigners and would like to kill us. And besides, the buildings in those other towns will be cold and dirty, crawling with disease. Oh, Jonathan!" She shook her head. "Just look at you. You almost died from typhoid, and you are not yet that strong."

"I'm all right, Rosalind," he said. "Don't use me for an excuse."

"But—but what about the children? We cannot lose another child."

To that, Jonathan Goforth made no quick response. He knew she had expressed her real fear, and the memory of their dear Florence was still painfully fresh to him, as well. Finally, after a long and respectful pause, he said, "I don't want to lose another child, either, my dear. But do you remember how the Lord delivered us from the Boxers? Think of the angry mobs that attacked us but could not kill us. Think of the mayor's scheme to have us ambushed on the road at night and how it miraculously failed. We traveled hundreds and hundreds of miles and could have been killed at any point. I am absolutely convinced that God was saving us for His purposes."

In a soft, reconciling voice, Mrs. Goforth said, "I don't doubt that, Jonathan, and I thank Him for it every day. But on the other hand, I don't think we should take foolish chances."

"You're right," said Mr. Goforth, leaning forward eagerly. "And that's what I've been realizing: We are never safer than when we are in the center of God's will! As long as He has a job for us, nothing can destroy us. And that's why . . . that's why I think our children are safest with us while we are following His plan. And I am convinced this is God's plan for reaching this part of China."

Fu-lin could feel tension fill the room, like air stretching a balloon.

"Well, I'm not convinced that we should be dragging our children all over the countryside exposing them to disease and harsh conditions," Rosalind Goforth said indignantly. "I intend to stay right here and turn this into a suitable and safe home for them."

In spite of Mrs. Goforth's intentions to protect her children, the very next day little Wallace—not yet three years old—became ill. For two weeks the child's life hung in the balance. Though Nurse Chang was the primary person helping Mrs. Goforth, Fu-lin stayed close, too, ready to run an errand, do laundry, or stoke up the fire whenever asked.

Although Mr. Goforth continued to meet with his evangelistic team getting ready for their first trip, he spent long hours at night nursing Wallace. Fu-lin watched the missionary's face. Had he changed his ideas about the children? Did he now agree that they should remain home?

Apparently not. When Wallace finally recovered and Jonathan was packing to leave on his first tour, he turned to Mrs. Goforth. "Come with me, Rose," he begged. "We must put God first and trust *Him* to protect our children. God can and will keep the children if we trust Him and step out in faith."

She shook her head. "I cannot," she said with a sniff as she dabbed at the corners of her eyes with her handkerchief. "You go, and I'll stay here and care for the little ones."

Jonathan Goforth had only been gone one day when Fu-lin felt a hand shaking him awake during the night from a sound sleep. "Fu-lin? Fu-lin!" It was Mrs. Goforth.

Fu-lin pulled the mask over his face and sat up groggily.

"The baby is very sick—sicker than Wallace was," she said. "I cannot get her temperature to come down."

The baby? Now Fu-lin was wide awake. Baby Constance had been born while the Goforths were in Canada.

"Get dressed quickly," Mrs. Goforth begged. "You must go find Jonathan and ask him to return. I . . . I'm afraid she's going to die."

Chapter 10

A Second Chance

FU-LIN CAUGHT A RIDE on a farmer's cart and found Jonathan Goforth in a village only half a day's journey away. They both hurried back to Changte, but by the time they arrived, the baby had lost consciousness.

All night and through the next day, Jonathan, Rosalind, and Nurse Chang took turns holding the baby and bathing her with cool water, trying to help 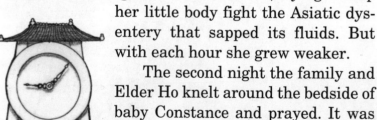 her little body fight the Asiatic dysentery that sapped its fluids. But with each hour she grew weaker.

The second night the family and Elder Ho knelt around the bedside of baby Constance and prayed. It was all they could do. Nurse Chang and

Fu-lin and a couple of the other Christians from the local church stood in the doorway of the darkened room and also prayed. The baby was having trouble breathing. Each rise of her little chest to gasp just one more breath came farther and farther apart. And then she lay completely motionless and silent.

Fu-lin listened to the clock on the wall count the seconds with its loud ticktock. Wasn't someone going to do something? Constance wasn't breathing any longer. But there was nothing more anyone could do. Finally Mr. Goforth leaned forward and pulled the sheet up over the little body. Mrs. Goforth stifled a cry by clasping her fist to her mouth.

Four-year-old Ruth, who was the oldest child in Paul and Helen's absence, began to whimper, and Mr. Goforth picked her up and comforted her. The silence continued without anyone moving as everyone stared at the little mound under the white sheet.

Finally Rosalind burst forth: "I couldn't do it. I couldn't protect my children. It was an impossible task." Mr. Goforth put his other arm around her as loud, wrenching sobs poured out, on and on and on until Fu-lin felt very uncomfortable.

Noticing him squirm and look around, Nurse Chang said, "It's all right, boy. She needs to cry. We all need to grieve."

Once again, the next day, the family and several of the local believers stood around a new grave in the Goforths' growing cemetery. Even with tears in her eyes, Rosalind spoke in a clear, calm voice. "One thing seems plain to me at this point: I must follow where God should lead. He must come first. I was trying to do God's job of protecting my children. That was an impossible task." And then she began to pray, "O God, I will trust You. I will go where You want me to go and leave the care of my children in Your hands."

Up until this point, Fu-lin had also thought the idea of taking the children on the evangelistic tours was foolish. He couldn't believe that it made any sense to take small children from town to town, "camping out" in strange places. But Fu-lin was just a house servant, so no one had asked for his opinion. Besides, he admitted to himself, heeding his own fears had not proved the best approach at Nanyangfu. In fact, he had shown himself to be more of a coward than a wise person. The faith of Mr. Goforth—that had proved to be wisest of all.

But traveling—that was still something he wanted to do! The last trip had not worked out as planned. But now, when the Boxers weren't stirring up riots . . .

He watched forlornly as the Goforths quickly packed clothes for the children and enough bedding, pots and pans, and household goods to set up temporary housekeeping. What would he do now that the Goforths were leaving for many months? He didn't blame them for not taking him along. Even though no one had accused him of abandoning the missionaries in Nanyangfu, why should they trust him now if the missionaries got in a tight spot?

"Fu-lin?" Mrs. Goforth said. "Why are you just standing there?"

"Excuse me, honorable lady," he said quickly. "I will help carry your bags out to the cart—"

"No, I mean, why aren't you packing your clothes? Mr. Goforth wants to leave as soon as possible. Have you gotten your mother's permission yet?"

Fu-lin didn't stop to think much about why the Goforths invited him to accompany them on the evangelism tour. Maybe they just needed a helper and would rather take someone who was already familiar to the family. It didn't matter. He felt blessed by God just to be along, visiting the many towns and villages north of Changte, doing whatever he was asked without complaining.

And the evangelistic plan God had given Jonathan Goforth seemed blessed by God, too. In every city and town where they stayed for a month, there were new converts, and a small church was established by the time they left.

Though some of their temporary houses were filthy and dingy—just as Mrs. Goforth had predicted—nevertheless, everyone's health remained strong. But one day, Rosalind discovered that, without knowing it, little Ruth had played all day long with another child who had the dreaded smallpox.

Smallpox was so common, so infectious, and so deadly that Chinese people sometimes said, "You might as well not even count a child until it survives small-pox."

"What'll we do?" moaned Mrs. Goforth. "This is what I feared most."

"We'll do the only thing we can do," said Jonathan. "We'll pray. Only God can protect her. But let's not forget, God is the best protector."

Each day for the next two and a half weeks, Mr. Goforth prayed for protection from the terrible disease. Each day Fu-lin made sure he was nearby when the girl woke up in the morning and Mrs. Goforth checked her for a fever. Each day she woke up bright and cheerful. At the breakfast table on the nineteenth day, Mrs. Goforth announced meekly, "The danger period has passed. You were right, Jonathan. God is our great Protector!"

Fu-lin didn't know which was the more astonishing—that little Ruth had not come down with the smallpox, or that after that, Rosalind Goforth seemed completely relieved of her fears for her children.

The road over the mountains from Hantan to the town of Wuan was so rough and rocky that everyone except the cart driver had to walk. Mr. Goforth and Fu-lin—who, at the age of sixteen now, was the size of some men—walked on either side of the cart, helping its wheels roll over the boulders in the road.

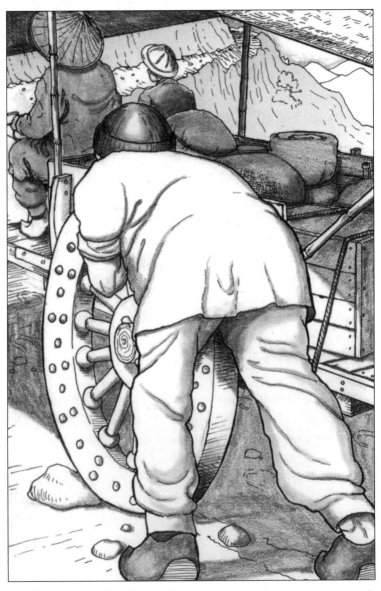

"Fu-lin," Mr. Goforth said as he stood up to catch his breath after helping the cart over a particularly rough stretch, "how would you like to give your testimony at our evangelistic meeting in Wuan?"

Fu-lin didn't answer. He wiped the sweat from his brow with his arm. It was Mr. Goforth's practice on this trip to invite new converts to give their testimony the very next night. He had once said, "It's the first step in training them to share the Good News with others." Fu-lin had become a Christian years earlier as a young boy—shortly after he began attending the mission school. But he had never given his testimony. He couldn't imagine standing up in front of strangers and talking. They wouldn't even hear what he had to say; instead, they'd be wondering what he was hiding behind his mask.

Besides, he didn't feel worthy to give his testimony now, not after deserting the missionaries at Nanyangfu during the Boxer Rebellion.

Seeing his hesitation, Mr. Goforth said, "Well, think about it. I'll ask you later."

The next day when Mr. Goforth brought it up again, Fu-lin just shook his head. Several more times Mr. Goforth invited Fu-lin to give his testimony while they were in that town, but Fu-lin always declined.

Soon their month in Wuan was nearly up, and it was time to prepare to move south to Hotsun. But the evangelist that they had left in the city of Hantan had not yet caught up with them. "We still have three more nights of meetings here," said Mr. Goforth to his wife one evening at dinner. "It would leave us shorthanded to send one of the other evangelists on ahead to make arrangements and find us a building to rent, but we've got to send someone."

Fu-lin, eating as he usually did in the next room, pricked up his ears.

Suddenly, Mr. Goforth switched from Chinese to English, apparently forgetting that Fu-lin could overhear them and understood English quite well. "Rosalind," he said, "could you do without Fu-lin for a few days? I'm thinking about sending him on ahead to arrange for our housing and other details."

"Oh, Jonathan," she said, "that's too much for him. It could be dangerous. We don't know how the people in Hotsun will receive us. Remember what happened the last time we sent him on a dangerous mission?"

"That was a couple of years ago, Rosalind. He's on his way to becoming a man, and I think he needs a second chance."

"A second chance at what?"

"At handling our trust in him."

"I don't know, Jonathan. He deserted us once. What if he lets us down again? Even the apostle Paul didn't want to take John Mark on a second journey after he had deserted them the first time. Now we've brought Fu-lin along—that's a second chance in itself, so why test him beyond what he can handle? He has not yet found the courage to give his testimony."

His rice seemed to stick in Fu-lin's throat. So. They did think he had deserted them. Now he knew.

"That's true," he heard Jonathan Goforth say.

"But I'd still like to give him a second chance."

A second chance! Fu-lin set down his chopsticks and retied his mask. If he got a second chance, this time he would not let them down.

Chapter 11

The Underground Boxers

HOTSUN WAS A CROWDED LITTLE TOWN with very few vacant buildings. The only one Fu-lin found had pigpens on both sides of the house, but they were not the only cause of the choking smells. A cloud of sulfur smoke hung over the town from all of the family-run pottery factories. Cheap coal with a high sulfur content was used in the furnaces to glaze the pottery.

In the one house Fu-lin did find for rent, there were eight large vats of fermenting cabbage. Like most Chinese, Fu-lin enjoyed eating cabbage in small quantities, but in large amounts ... well, between the smells of the fermenting cabbage, the pigs, and the sulfur smoke, Fu-lin nearly threw up the small lunch he had eaten an hour earlier.

He finally located the owner of the building, who turned out to be a Mr. Tao. He was working in his open storefront a short distance away. "Good afternoon, Mr. Tao. How much are you asking to rent your building down the street?" Fu-lin asked the landlord.

The man looked up and jumped back with a little cry. "Do not rob, please," he said, throwing up his hands and dropping the cloth he had been arranging on a display table.

"No, no, I'm not a bandit," said Fu-lin, putting his hand to his mask.

"Then why wear that awful thing?" The man picked up the cloth and began folding it.

"I beg your pardon," said Fu-lin with a bow. "I was just wanting to ask about renting your house." He pointed down the street.

"Who's renting it? For how long?" asked the landlord. He was a small man with a wispy white moustache and beard and a long gray pigtail hanging down his back from under the black pillbox cap on his head.

"Mr. and Mrs. Goforth, their family, and their assistants. I'm one of their assistants," Fu-lin added proudly.

"Are these foreigners?" the man asked, squinting his eyes.

Fu-lin cleared his throat. "They are missionaries, very good people."

"I don't rent to foreigners," said the man and turned back to his merchandise.

"Wait," said Fu-lin. "This is just for a short time—

one month, even less. I'm sure no one else would rent your house, and they would pay a fair price."

"I do not rent to foreigners." The man's voice suddenly got louder as though he were announcing his comments to everyone on the street. "We do not want foreign devils in our town! We do not want traitors in our town!" Each statement got louder until three passersby had stopped to observe the dispute. "Get out while you can, and never come back!"

After looking from one observer to another, hoping one of them would speak up on his behalf, Fu-lin walked away from the store. Without thinking, he headed back to the vacant house. In spite of the smells, he stood out front staring into the house's open front door and then up and down the street. He had asked around, and this had been the only place for rent that anyone had mentioned. Maybe he just needed to walk the streets and see for himself if he could find some other vacant building. It wouldn't have to be a house. The Goforths had made do with a warehouse in one town, a barn in another, and an empty store in another town. But Mrs. Goforth hated those makeshift arrangements. They seldom provided privacy, and in bad weather—either heat or cold—they were no substitute for a real house. He had so wanted to get them a good place to live. He didn't want to let Mrs. or Mr. Goforth down.

Fu-lin began walking slowly, trying to think of some other method for finding a house to rent until he finally settled into a serious search. Up one street and down the next he trudged. Any place that looked unused—weeds growing through the steps, no children, smoke, or action—any clue that a place might be vacant, he investigated, but the only thing he found was an empty shed with one side completely open.

Evening was coming, and he didn't know who owned the shed, but because it was open, he wandered in. The place was empty except for a pile of dusty straw mats in the corner and a few empty boxes. He sat down on one of the boxes and picked up a handful of pebbles from the dirt floor. One at a time he tossed them toward the post that held up the roof on the open side. They could hang quilts over that opening and build a little cooking stove in the center if they could find some bricks, but with a dirt floor and no sleeping kang, Mrs. Goforth would be furious. How could she care for the children here? How would she ever have her women's meetings in a place like this? Where would they hold their evening evangelistic meetings? This was not suitable. The Goforths would be arriving the next day, and he had failed to find them a place to live.

Failed again!

He stood up and threw the remaining pebbles with all his might at the back wall of the shed. They clattered to the ground as he stomped out and set off down the darkening street. His stomach growled. From a street vendor he bought an oiled paper cone of dough strings and, not really caring where he was going, wandered into a narrow alley.

Whap! The cone of dough strings flew from his stinging fingers and splattered on the wall.

"What do you think you are doing here? Do you
think you are some kind of bandit wearing that

foolish mask?" The breath of the man who had slapped his hand stank of cheap rice wine. He was a hard-looking man with the front half of his head shaved back to above his ears and a pigtail gathered from the hair in the back. He was also missing an eye, and he had healed in such a way that there wasn't even a scar or an eyebrow, simply smooth skin all the way down the right side of his face. Two other men closed in behind Fu-lin, each carrying a thin bamboo cane. The one-eyed man snorted. "Bandit or not, you don't seem to take advice very well. We don't want any foreign devils in our town, and we don't want any of their stooges here, either. I think Mr. Tao made that quite clear to you this afternoon, so why are you still here?" He gave Fu-lin such a hard shove that he would have fallen down if one of the men behind him had not given him an equally hard shove back the other way.

Fu-lin's head snapped back and forth painfully with the pushing. "Leave me alone," he protested. "I haven't done anything to you."

"You were told to leave town, but you ignored the warning. No one ignores the Boxers."

Fu-lin felt a stab of fear. "Boxers? But—"

The man with the scar laughed. "So you thought the Boxers disappeared! It will take more than a stupid law on paper to root out our underground society. As long as there are foreigners, we will keep fighting. You were foolish to ignore Mr. Tao's warning. Now you will pay."

With that, one of the bamboo canes landed a

stinging blow across Fu-lin's back. The other whipped across the back of his legs, and then the blows rained down so rapidly that Fu-lin couldn't count them. All he knew was that he was soon on the ground writhing in pain.

"Enough," said the one-eyed man. "We wouldn't want him to have any trouble walking out of town . . . *tonight!*" He spat out that last word. And then the three men disappeared as quickly as they had come.

The alley was quiet. Fu-lin sat up, checking his arms and legs as he choked back a sob. Mr. Goforth had said he was becoming a man, so he would not let himself bawl like a baby. Nothing seemed broken. Welts were appearing wherever the canes had hit him, but he was not bleeding.

As he readjusted his mask, he looked around. Maybe he ought to get out of Hotsun like the man had ordered. But in the same instant, he remembered that Mr. Goforth had said, *"As long as we are doing God's work, God will protect us."* Paul the apostle had been beaten and stoned many times, but God had protected him. The Goforths had escaped the Boxers. The children had been protected from disease. Therefore, he—Fu-lin the Wolf Boy—would not run away, *not this time.* He would stay and do his best and trust God for the rest. He might not have a house for the Goforths when they arrived tomorrow, but he would be there to meet them.

He got up and checked the dough strings. Most were so covered with dirt that he couldn't eat them. But a couple remained in the bottom of the paper cone. He dug them out with his fingers and stuffed them in his mouth as he limped down the alley. When he got to the street, it took him a few minutes to figure out where he was, since he had been wandering aimlessly before the attack. Once he got his bearings, he headed off with purpose.

It was now dark, and there were few lamps along the streets. Mostly he found his way by the dim light that shone from people's windows and a yellow moon that had risen into the sky like a glowing paper lantern.

Fu-lin turned into the open shed he'd found earlier. In the dark corner he found the straw mats and shook the dust out of them. Something scurried across the floor and out of the shed—probably a rat. Fu-lin curled his aching body up on the mats and soon fell into a troubled sleep.

He awoke with his heart pounding. It was light outside, but his dream had come again. It was the same as before, falling, falling down into the dark cave where the dust and horrible smell had almost overwhelmed him. He heard the low growl and saw the yellow eyes dancing back and forth. But he had not woken up then as he usually did. He had stayed in the dream, and the terrible thing that was always just about to happen had been as bad as he'd ever expected. His thundering heart testified to his fright . . . but he was alive. Alive! He had lived through the dream, and now he could remember it all.

He jumped up and then lurched as his bruised and sore body reminded him of the beating the night before. More cautiously, he went outside and began walking the streets of Hotsun again, looking for an empty house that the Goforths could rent. They would arrive about noon, and he must be ready to meet them.

Chapter 12

The Man Behind the Mask

THE NOON SUN WAS HIGH OVERHEAD, and Fu-lin was waiting under a eucalyptus tree at the edge of town along the road from Wuan. His shoulders slumped, and his head hung slightly forward. He had not run away, but he had not succeeded in his assignment, either. What would Mr. Goforth say? What would *Mrs.* Goforth say? She was the one who thought he wasn't up to the task. Still, he had not deserted them, even when the Boxers threatened. He stood by the road, waiting to face their disappointment like a man.

Over the small rise a quarter of a mile from town, two mule carts appeared. They carried the Goforths, Nurse

Chang, the new Bible woman, and the Chinese evangelists that made up the team. Slowly they approached, and Fu-lin stepped out from where he had been leaning against the tree and waved.

Mr. Goforth and one of the evangelists hopped down from the cart. "Take me, Daddy, take me," squealed four-year-old Ruth. She was standing on the driver's seat, dancing with excitement as she leaned far out and stretched her arms toward her father. Mr. Goforth lifted her down and then held her hand as she skipped along beside him, past the slow-moving carts toward Fu-lin.

"Good morning, honorable sir," Fu-lin said with a little bow.

Mr. Goforth bowed back. "It is very good to see you, Fu-lin. What do you think of this little town of Hotsun? It seems like we've been smelling it for the last three miles." He looked toward the town. "It's not cold yet; why is there so much smoke?"

Eager to discuss anything other than his failures, Fu-lin responded, "That's from the pottery kilns. There's good clay in the hills around here, and many people have little pottery factories."

"Oh yes. They do make a lot of fine pottery in this region." He looked back at Fu-lin. "Have you found a suitable place for us to live and have our meetings?"

Fu-lin dropped his eyes to the ground where his right foot absently kicked back and forth in the dust. "Not exactly, sir," he mumbled. "There's one terrible house, but the owner won't rent it. And I did find a vacant shed. It's large enough, but one side is completely open—no wall."

By then the carts were passing. Mr. Goforth sighed deeply and started walking with Ruth skipping alongside. "Well, let's go see what we can do," he said over his shoulder to Fu-lin.

Fu-lin swung in behind him, still limping from the caning of the night before. The missionary never yelled at people, but Fu-lin could tell from the way his eyes had squinted slightly and how the muscles along the side of his jaws had throbbed that Mr. Goforth was very disappointed in him.

Once they had stabled the mules at an inn—where they also left the children, Nurse Chang, and the other members of the team—Fu-lin led Mr. and Mrs. Goforth to the one house he had found.

"This will never do," announced Mrs. Goforth with a handkerchief over her mouth to block some of the smell from the pigs and the cabbage vats. She immediately began walking away.

Mr. Goforth was gagging, too, as he followed her. "I guess that mask of yours comes in handy sometimes," he said to Fu-lin, trying to lighten the atmosphere of disappointment. When they had caught up to Mrs. Goforth, he said, "Maybe we shouldn't be too hasty. Possibly we can get the owner to move those vats, and—"

"Never," interrupted Mrs. Goforth. "Besides, didn't Fu-lin say it wasn't for rent?" She looked at Fu-lin.

"Yes, but . . ." began Mr. Goforth. He turned to Fu-lin. "What did you mean by that? What did the man *actually* say?"

Fu-lin reported his conversation with Mr. Tao, including the warning against foreigners and the demand that he get out of town.

"Well, I wouldn't worry about that . . . and I'm glad you didn't!" Mr. Goforth smiled at Fu-lin and clapped him on the shoulder reassuringly. He happened to hit one of the painful bruises, and Fu-lin winced and dropped his shoulder a little.

"What's the matter?" asked Mrs. Goforth. "Have you had an accident or something? I've noticed you limping, and now you act as though your shoulder is hurt."

Reluctantly, Fu-lin told about the attack in the alley. "I think they were Boxers, or at least they had the same attitude toward foreigners. They were very bad men. I'll never forget the one-eyed man, the one who slapped the dough strings out of my hand."

Mr. Goforth nodded, and a quiet smile spread across his face. "Speaking of dough strings," he said, "I think we need some lunch. Let's go find that street vendor."

They found the vendor right in the center of town in an open area where several merchants had set up booths to sell their goods. The vendor had no sooner handed them their bowls of rice and vegetables than a crowd of curious people began to gather around the foreigners. "Why are you white devils here?" "Where have you come from?" "You can't curse us with your foreign magic. Be gone!" The comments came from every side.

"Pray with your eyes open," Mr. Goforth instructed in English. "Otherwise they may think we are trying to cast a spell on them." A moment later he said to his wife, "I think we'd better get back to the inn. It isn't safe standing on the street with no place to go. Fu-lin, we *need* a headquarters. Please try once more to locate a place to rent. We'll be praying for your success."

Fu-lin went one way, while the Goforths went the other.

Fu-lin ran his fingers through his hair as he walked. He had been up and down every street in the town and nothing seemed vacant. What else could he do?

Then just ahead of him, a man came out of a gate in a well-maintained garden wall. He was dressed in fine clothes, and suddenly Fu-lin walked faster to catch up with him. Wealthy people were likely to own property. He had looked everywhere, but he had asked very few people for help after the scolding Mr. Tao had given him.

"Begging your pardon, most honorable sir," Fu-lin said, touching the man's sleeve.

The man turned and then shied back with his hands up to protect himself the moment he saw the Wolf Boy.

Fu-lin stopped and put his hand to his mask. "Forgive me," he said, bowing. "I mean you no harm. I wear this only because . . . because of my face. But I do have a request to make of you. Do you know of anyone in town who might have a house for rent?"

The man quickly shook his head and looked as though he were about to walk on, but Fu-lin quickly explained why he was looking for a rental house. And the more he talked, the more interested the man appeared.

"My sister in Hantan tells me she has become a Christian," the man said. "Her letters sound as though she is very excited, but I do not understand this new religion. I would be interested in talking to your Mr. Goforth. Maybe he can help me understand."

A half hour later, Fu-lin came running into the inn excitedly calling, "Mr. Goforth! Mr. Goforth! A wealthy man has offered you a fine empty house that has just been cleaned and redecorated. He fixed it up for a nobleman who is due to come through here next month. But until then you can have it for as long as you like—rent free!"

That night they held their first evangelistic meeting in Hotsun. Even on such short notice the room was filled with curious people. After some singing and an explanation by Mr. Goforth that they were there to tell about Jesus Christ, he said, "And now I want you to hear the testimony of one of our evangelists and how Jesus has changed his life."

He nodded to the Chinese evangelist who was

scheduled to speak, but before the man could rise to his feet, Fu-lin jumped up and said in a loud but squeaky voice, "Yes, I want to tell my story and how Jesus has given me courage."

Mr. Goforth looked startled but made no move to stop him. Fu-lin opened his mouth, then hesitated. Standing in the back of the room was the one-eyed man whose henchmen had given him such a beating the night before. Fu-lin swallowed as he stared into the man's shining eye not twenty feet away. Had Jesus really given him enough courage to face this evil man?

"In . . . in my hometown of Changte, I am called W-Wolf Boy," he stammered, staring the man right in the eye. "My parents were very poor. My father was a woodcutter, and we—my whole family—often went with him to the forest.

"One day when I was six, I wandered away when I was supposed to be helping my mother gather mushrooms. Suddenly, I stumbled and fell down a concealed hole into what turned out to be a wolf den. It was dark and filled with dust and smelled like urine and dead animal carcasses. As I sat up, I heard growling and snarling, and then I saw pairs of yellow eyes in the dark."

The eye of the man in the back of the room was just about as frightening as the eyes of those wolves, but Fu-lin gritted his teeth and continued. "I had invaded their den where they were protecting their pups, and in an instant, they attacked me. I tried to protect myself with my arms, but one got a strong bite on the side of my face and wouldn't let go until my flesh tore away.

"By the time my parents heard my screaming and came to rescue me, I had been severely injured. They took me to the hospital at Mr. and Mrs. Goforth's mission station. There the doctor worked over me for many hours. They did all they could, but my face remained badly disfigured. That is why I am called Wolf Boy."

He looked around at Mrs. Goforth, who was smiling encouragingly from her seat at the little portable pump organ. "At the hospital," he continued, "I learned about Jesus and asked Him to come into my life and forgive my sins. When I recovered enough to go to the mission school, I put on a mask because I didn't want the other children to see how I looked.

"Some years later, when my father died, I went to work for the Goforths so that I could pay for my education and live with them. I still work for them, and that is why I'm here tonight."

He stopped and looked around. This was the really hard part, but he would not quit again. "The fear of that wolf attack stayed with me for years. I had nightmares about it that filled me with dread—fear that worse things were going to happen to me." Fulin then stared right at the one-eyed man. "And when the Boxers attacked the Goforths outside Nanyangfu, I became so scared that I ran away and deserted them. But . . . today Jesus has given me new courage. I now trust Him to be my Protector, and I know that no one—*no one*—can kill me as long as God wants me alive. I feel afraid sometimes, but I no longer am ruled by fear!"

Fu-lin took a deep breath. "I can even thank God for the attack by those wolves because, if that had not happened to me, I would never have come to know Jesus in the mission hospital. I can thank God for this." With a quick movement, Fu-lin reached up and slipped off his mask.

There was a gasp from some of the people in the room as they saw his deformed face with its ugly scars. Others murmured quietly to one another, but Fu-lin was smiling as well as his crooked face would allow.

At that moment Mrs. Goforth began pumping mightily on the little organ, and squeaky notes poured out as she began singing in Chinese . . .

"Down at the cross where my Savior died,
Down where for cleansing from sin I cried,
There to my heart was the blood applied;
Glory to His name!"

By then Fu-lin, Mr. Goforth, and all the evangelists had joined in the singing.

When they finished, Mr. Goforth stood up and said, "Thank you, thank you, Mr. Chou. I think we all appreciated that testimony."

As Fu-lin sat down, he realized that Mr. Goforth had called him by his family name. He was no longer the Wolf Boy or even just Fu-lin. He was now "*Mr. Chou*"—not the boy, but the *man* behind the mask. And he would never hide behind it again.

More About
Jonathan and Rosalind Goforth

WHEN YOUNG JONATHAN GOFORTH arrived at Knox College in Toronto, Ontario, Canada, his classmates teased him cruelly. Born February 2, 1859, he had grown up as a poor farm boy. He wore shabby clothes and didn't understand city ways. To improve his appearance at college, he bought some cloth, but before he could get it sewn into new clothes, his fellow students woke him up in the middle of the night. They tied it around his neck like a cape and made him run up and down the dorm hallway, poking fun at him.

They may have laughed at him then, but before he graduated in 1886, his classmates came to respect him so much that they raised the money to send him to China as a missionary. They had seen his sincerity in preaching at rescue missions in Toronto, visiting prisons, and witnessing door-to-door.

The following year Jonathan met and married Rosalind Bell Smith, an attractive, talented, and well-educated woman who had been born (May 6, 1864) and raised in London, England, in a wealthy family.

In 1888 the Goforths sailed for China, where Jonathan found the Chinese language particularly difficult to learn as they attempted to adjust to a new culture. Over the years they had eleven children and suffered the sorrow of seeing five of them die very young.

A powerful evangelist, Jonathan became known as the "flaming preacher," sometimes speaking to as many as twenty-five thousand at a time. But the Goforths also used what they called "open-house" evangelism. The Chinese people were curious about how they lived, especially some of their furnishings like a kitchen stove, a sewing machine, and an organ. So they arranged tours of their house all day long. Before they would take a group of fifty people through the house, Rosalind would preach to the women, and Jonathan would preach to the men.

By 1900 an organized uprising known as the Boxer Rebellion had spread throughout China. Its purpose was to drive all foreigners from the country. The Chinese empress encouraged it because Japanese and Western outsiders seemed to be taking over the country. Thousands of foreigners were killed, and the Goforths fled a thousand miles across China to escape. On the way, an angry crowd of men attacked Jonathan and nearly beat him to death with a sword.

When they returned to China about a year later, their approach changed to a traveling evangelistic ministry that produced more than thirteen thousand converts between 1908 and 1913 alone.

The Goforths worked in China for forty-six years before poor health forced them to return to Canada in 1934. In addition to their many converts, they trained sixty-one full-time Chinese evangelists and Bible teachers and established thirty mission stations.

Jonathan died on October 8, 1936, and Rosalind joined him in heaven on May 31, 1942.

For Further Reading

Goforth, Rosalind. *Climbing: Memories of a Missionary Wife*. Grand Rapids, Mich.: Zondervan Publishing House, 1940.

_____. *Goforth of China*. Grand Rapids, Mich.: Zondervan Publishing House, 1937.

_____. *Jonathan Goforth* (*Goforth of China* retold for today's readers). Minneapolis: Bethany House Publishers, 1986.

Goforth, Rosalind and Jonathan. *Miracle Lives of China*. Grand Rapids, Mich.: Zondervan Publishing House, 1931.

Geographical Names in China

SINCE 1949 THE CHINESE GOVERNMENT has been working to standardize the language used throughout its country. Instead of different dialects for different regions, *Putonghua* ("standard speech") is being used everywhere. Westerners recognize it as Mandarin, the dialect of North China. Within China, this has resulted in a standard way to say various place-names.

In addition, in 1977 the Chinese government asked all members of the United Nations to employ phonetic spelling (or *pinyin*) any time the Latin alphabet is used for place-names in China. The result of these two efforts has been the seeming change in many names for Chinese cities, towns, provinces, rivers, etc.

In this book we have used the old spelling, because that is the way the Goforths would have said and spelled those names. However, if you are trying to find these places on a modern map, you will want to look for the new names. Some are the same, some are similar, and some look very different.

Old		New
Old		**New**
Changte	=	Anyang
Chefoo	=	Yantai
Chengchow	=	Zhengzhou
Chuwang	=	Chuwang
Fancheng	=	Xiangfan
Hankow	=	Wuhan
Hantan	=	Handan
Honan	=	Henan Province
Hopei	=	Hebi
Hotsun	=	Hecun
Hsintien	=	Xindian
Kaifengfu	=	Kaifeng
Nanyangfu	=	Nanyang
Peking	=	Beijing
Pengcheng	=	Pengcheng
Tientsin	=	Tianjin
Wuan	=	Wu'an
Yellow River	=	Huang He

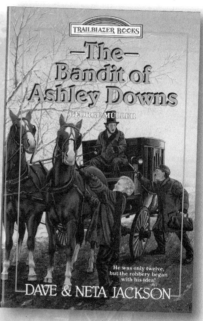

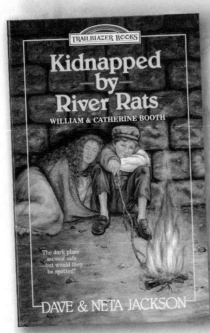